The Rivers Daughter

S. S. Nightshade

For everyone who played mermaids in the

summer as a kid.

Yes, they have color changing tails!

Trigger Warning/Content Disclaimer

Intended for readers 18+

All characters are 18+

- Blood drinking/Bloodlust
- Explicit fighting sequences and death scenes
- Explicit sexual scenes: during emotional breakdowns or for manipulative purposes
- Explicit, vulgar and/or derogatory language

Please note: this author took creative liberty with the descriptions of various elements of North American folklore, history and geography. These representations are completely fictional and do not claim to be accurate representations of any specific lore or fact.

Prologue

Renita

Not many things are as old as my kin, but the Appalachian Mountains are a close second. I've often wondered if that's part of the reason I've been able to settle here so easily. If my ancient blood had recognized something in the mountains dust. It's one of the only plausible explanations for why a being from the sea could survive here with little stress. Well, that and the Witches.

The river town of Sashomik was a desolate, grey place in the winter. Its residents preferred to huddle inside the warmth of their cottages, reveling in the privacy that the warmer seasons didn't offer. Even barely into the last week of May, tourists would begin to flock in.

Only three hours from the Big Apple, and less than one from Philadelphia, put us in quite the desirable spot on the map for city slickers. The town was nestled in the shadow of the Appalachian Mountain train, and surrounded by miles of woodland and open meadows, making it the nature lovers dream. Hiking, horseback riding, ziplining, bird watching, hunting, four wheeling— you name it and the town had it nearby. With the Lehigh River weaving its way through its center, the added enjoyment of various watersports drew in even more people.

Now, if you've experienced rural Pennsylvania, you'll know those activities are quite widespread throughout the region. What makes our little town different? Again, the Witches. Which no one realizes are here of course.

Most of the residents of the town are a mixture of Salem and New Orleans descendants. These Northern and Southern staples of American ghost stories and magic have converged at the base of these ancient mountains, the mix of powerful bloodlines now calling this place home. Maybe like me, something in their bones recognized this place, or perhaps it all just happened by chance.

To the modern world they are farmers, craftsmen, carpenters and schoolteachers, but to the hidden network of the old world, they are the epicenter of water magic. They've become so skilled and strong because they shared everything with each other, and educated those who were brave enough to travel here. Gatekeeping was a crime severe enough for banishment.

Practices and spells were enthusiastically woven together between different heritages, strengthening the network of magic as a whole. The voodoo rain dances of the bayou were combined with the siphoning rituals of New

England. A Warrior's strength could increase after deepening their empathetic reach. Likewise, the more emotionally charged practitioners were able to increase their defensive spells after studying under the guidance of a Warrior and would no longer need to rely on a Witch of a different skillset to maintain their safety.

The only thing that didn't change, especially with the water, was the skillsets themselves. Everyone's practice could grow stronger, but they could not learn a new type of magic. You were either a Siphon, a Manipulative, an Empath, or a Warrior. The water is stubborn that way.

Eventually, the town's magical influence grew so much that the rest of the old world began to follow its lead. A very small, very private, University opened at the edge of the town, housing a variety of magical youth to practice their skills. Witches, Nymphs, Vampires and Fae—but not the Mer.

Though they were too prideful to have their youth taught by land dwellers, they were smart enough to recognize the growing power and formed an alliance. At first, the Witches had been surprised. The world of magic was already private, but the Mer took it to an entirely different level. Submerged beneath the sea, they were completely disconnected and preferred it that way. But their mounting problems drove them to seek like-minded individuals.

There is a difference between a Mer and a Siren. A Mer can produce magic equal to that of the power of a hundred Witches but must abide by the same rule of water. They too could only be a Siphon, Manipulative, Warrior, or Empath. They could just slightly mix, or branch into another magic, but the spell would drain them. If they survived it, they wouldn't have magic for the rest of their lives.

Being born in the water, it made sense they could use it with less effort. The Witches believed the rule still applying to the Mer was the Goddess' way of maintaining balance between Land and Sea. Though one could overpower the other, it depended on who had what skill, ensuring the balance didn't tip fully in the Mers favor.

But the rule, for whatever reason, did not apply to Sirens. A Siren could manifest the power of a hundred Mer, in any form of magic they wished. Depending on their years and ability to control their power, it could require an army to take down just one. It had before.

They were very rare, and a threat to the Mers carefully concealed life. Human waste was a constant threat to the species, for magic could not clean the sea. And a Sirens hunger brought in a different threat altogether: science.

On more than one occasion over the centuries, a Sirens song would lure humans towards a hidden cove, allowing them to breach the magical barrier. And humans, seeing the mythical creature, became obsessed. Mer were hunted, slaughtered, caught, and experimented on. The Witches understood what the Mer were suffering all too well. After all, humanity's morbid curiosity and narrow-minded thinking had killed thousands of their own kin over the centuries.

And so, if a Mer manifested a Sirens power, they were banished for the safety of their people. If they resisted, they were killed, because a Siren could not resist the pull of their power any more than a human could.

The Witches aided the Mer by keeping their world hidden, as well as occasionally offering Warriors to deal with a rogue Siren or two who sought chaos. In return, the Mer funded the Witches every wish and necessity. It was unknown how, and the Witches having every worry removed, didn't feel the need to ask. It was a glorious partnership which never faltered.

At least not until I was born.

Renita

The shadows presence was constant every night, sometimes making it downright impossible to sleep. On the rare occasion I did block out his attention, rest continued to allude me, and I was embraced by nightmares instead. I frequently drowned in my sleep. Or fell from a cliff, like my mother had that stormy night fourteen years ago. That was the only time in my life that I felt the control on my powers slipping.

I knew the shadow was a he, because he always had to forcefully intervene. Or do something dramatic. Once he even dove off the cliff after me, the two of us falling so close I finally saw something through the dark around us. His eyes, a shade of lilac so soft they couldn't be anything but natural. As soon as I saw them, I would wake. Like today.

Humidity already clung to my skin even though the sun had yet to crest the ridge above. The dawn teased the edge of the black sky, in a shade so similar to his eyes that I found myself pausing at the water's edge.

I didn't have long until this very spot would be teeming with humans, so despite the lingering ache in my chest, I dropped my chemise and plunged into the frigid water. The shock of cold thoroughly extinguished any lingering sense of sleep, and mourning. And the familiar weight against my hips sent a thrill through me, as it always did.

A mermaid. A foolish one at that.

As if our town wasn't already searched with a fine-toothed comb because of all the magic, an accidental photoshoot with a drunken college student made the entire country buzz with excitement. Who didn't want to see a mermaid? And why was there one in a freshwater river in Pennsylvania of all places?

Year after year I found myself combating the hordes of little girls who flooded our streets hoping to catch a glimpse of the magical creature. Paired with that, I now received my annual chiding from my Aunt Cora.

She was the Witch who'd helped free me from the stormy waves and brought me here to live safely in the mountains shadow. The least I could do after my impromptu teenage mistake was withhold my complaints and allow her to fuss. Especially since I was reminded daily that her fears had merit.

A human's lust for knowledge knew no limits, whether financial or moral. With their advancing technology, and my lack of control at the time, I would have been hunted down within my first few days on land for certain.

Banishing my thoughts, I broke the surface of the river silently. The slow wave of my tail beneath me easily kept my head above water long enough to pretend to take a few breaths. Then I slunk under again, the caress of the rapids calming the remaining restlessness. No one was here yet. It was the week of the Water Festival, so everyone was out late drinking. Even the fishermen wouldn't be out for another half hour or so. I was safe.

Slowly, I made my way down into the belly of the river to my hiding place. The Witches could get down to it in an emergency, but it would be one hell of an impressive spell to manipulate this much moving water. Paired with the current, nearly twenty feet of water was intimidating enough for most land-dwellers to avoid. And even if they did decide to dive in, this spot was avoided because it was too dark, too slippery with mud, and too tangled with underwater roots. Too perfect for me to hide my treasures.

Growing up with my mother, it was typical to collect all manners of shiny trinkets. Jewelry, gems, coins, hair ornaments and the like. In the old days, we Mer needed good hiding places, often deep, to avoid the pirate raids. Their obsession with treasure, and their miserable attempt at keeping track of their own stores, was apparently their way of trying to bribe us onto land, while simultaneously competing with us for wealth. Needless to say, whatever treasure they carried on their vessels was retrieved once we sank them.

That was the old way, and something I hadn't been taught until I came here. Cora had always been adamant that I know of my heritage, my abilities, and my place in this word, despite the dangers it would bring. I was free to practice my magic as I wished, so long as there were no humans present, and at least two of the Covens leaders to reel me in if necessary.

My fingers dug into the silt of the riverbed, closing on protruding roots to hold me still as my eyes quickly adjusted to the dark. This wasn't originally my place of solace. After being spotted five years ago, it was an annual tradition for the human tourists to come and make offerings, like a wishing well. They would flip coins into the rushing water, drop old necklaces or pale white stones. The riverbed began to glitter like the stars in the sky, and so I decided to take my small box of treasures hidden beneath my floorboards and bring them to rest here as well.

My fingers grazed the pointed teeth of my mother's silver comb, before moving on to pluck a pair of jasper earrings out of an upturned freshwater clamshell. After securing them to my lobes I slowly moved down the line, swapping the lapis lazuli rings on my fingers for a few aquamarine ones.

Satisfied with my choices, I pumped my tail once, returning to the surface. The sun had crested the ridgeline by now, so I swam towards the willow grove. Cora had it specially planted after my arrival. It was on our private property so the tourists and fisherman couldn't walk through it. The thick drooping limbs reached the water's surface, making a natural privacy screen for me to enter and exit.

"You were out too late." Before I had even let the willow leaves fall shut behind me, I heard Clarice's voice ringing in my ears. She was Cora's daughter, two years younger than me, and always on my case. "Your scales glitter like damned diamonds in the sunlight. You know that Ren."

"It's okay, no one was out." I tried to give a reassuring smile, but she wasn't going to be subdued.

"Doesn't mean they don't have cameras set up. Or if some drunk decided to pass out on the riverbank hidden in the reeds, they could see you by accident."

I shook my head as I pulled myself onto the grassy bank, rolling to rest on my elbows. As much as I wanted to argue, she was right. Even in the willows shade, the scales on my arms were sparkling. But they were nothing compared to the striking silver of my tail.

Most Mer had scales that were various shades of blue or green, depending on where in the sea they were born. There were only a few vibrant colors such as mine.

What Cora knew was limited, but from what she gathered, the Goddess' determined what color a Mers scales would be. Blues and Greens were nothing to be ashamed of, as they were born a Mer and that was blessing enough. However, there were those with striking colors to signify specialized places in life. Red scales donned the diplomats and nobles. Black for Warriors, and Gold for priests and priestesses.

But no one knew what color tail a high-ranking royal would have. Some say they had a mirage of every color, others said they could shade-shift too remain hidden. The latter was the popular belief, assuming they would don a blue, green, or red tail to blend in for their own safety should they find themselves in the open sea alone.

The most interesting thing about it all, the only thing I genuinely liked about the Mer, was that their power and royalty was not determined by bloodline. Anyone could be born with any color tail. It was something outside of societal and biological control, left for the heavens to decide. A soul chosen, rather than a position inherited.

My tail, however, would be an alarm bell to any Mer that saw it. Cora had never heard of a silver-tailed Mer before. They didn't exist. And considering my mother's scales were black, it could only mean one thing that my powers later proved: I was a Siren.

I stared down at it for a moment longer, the scales glittering back up at me, before mumbling the incantation that had my lower body

going numb. A ripple in time, and then my scales
dulled and sank into my tanned legs. Clarice
tossed me my chemise, which I'd abandoned by
the tree trunk, and as I stood I slid it on over my
head.

"Thank you."

"I still think you need to be more careful,"
she mumbled, but the annoyance in her voice had
eased. She tossed her hair over her shoulder,
revealing a new, third piercing in her left ear that
my eyes snagged on.

"You know I'm far more open to your style
than your mother," I said with a frown. "But stop
stealing my pearls. They're rare."

"You never wear them, so I borrow them,"
she emphasized with a roll of her eyes. I stifled a
sigh. They did look good on her, their golden hue
pairing nicely with the set of two copper hoops she
currently donned, and deep turquoise of her hair.

Together, we brushed aside the willow
boughs and walked side by side back to the house.
It was an elegant spread, on a little patch of land
brimming with the vegetables and plants that
Cora grew to sell at the market. The dewdrops
hummed to life as we passed, slowly lifting into a
mist that enveloped Clarice. As a Manipulative,
the water was drawn to her, and she was still
learning how to control its attraction. She
released a string of curses as I gently waved my
palm over her, sending the water back to its perch
before we crossed the threshold.

"I could have done it," she protested, and I couldn't help but smirk.

"I know, but you just chastised me to be more careful, didn't you? Just returning the favor." She huffed in response, so I let it drop.

I entered my room off the kitchen, quickly changing into my work uniform and grabbing my keys. It was a little mundane, working at the diner, but a part of me enjoyed the simple reality of it. After all, nothing else in my life was simple.

"Don't be late to school," I reminded her on my way out. She rolled her eyes, wordlessly passing me my lunch but she let me press a light kiss to her cheek in farewell.

"Renita!" I hadn't made it more than three steps off our porch before a pair of women were marching towards me. I smiled, waiting to walk with them.

"Morning girls," I said warmly, sliding my sunglasses onto my face. Even after all the years on land, the sun still hurt my eyes on days like this. Cloudless, hot, and irritatingly bright.

The Witches often called them seafoam, somewhere between a light green and soft blue. I took their word for it; I'd never really seen the sea from above. I'd been under it the first ten years of my life, before dragging myself out of its boiling black waters onto a beach covered with shattered glass from lightning strikes.

"Rumor has it your Aunt has been called away for the day," Maria said by way of greeting.

"She seemed in quite a tizzy over it, with the water festival taking place and all."

"I think she was more worried about not being able to watch Ren here like a hawk." Alice shared a knowing smile with me. She was the first friend I'd made here, as she pretty much stalked me every time I left my room until I finally spoke to her. It was a horrible time, my first months here. The loneliness and the anger were so potent I sometimes believed they would eat me away. Or make me implode.

I wasn't a secret kept from the Witches; they all knew full well what I was for their own safety. Alice was the first to push my boundaries, and quite literally pushed me into the water, revealing my tail. She was also the first to take a direct hit from my power– something I was reminded of to this day each time I saw the curling silver scar peek out from beneath her shirts collar.

"That too," Maria admitted, drawing me from my darkening thoughts.

The diner was only a few blocks from the house, situated between a magic shop and one of the kayak rental booths. Though it had expansive indoor seating, most of our guests would flock to the outdoor patio backed up against the river. Our locals were usually the only ones who would eat inside, and be here by opening time for breakfast. Just a few blissful hours before the tourists would wake up and pour in for brunch. Today however, seemed to be an exception.

"Are we late or something?" Alice asked, as we quickly shimmied our way through the growing crowd outside. Tamara, our manager, somehow managed to crack the door open far enough to usher us inside.

"Not technically, but we did have a reservation."

"A reservation?" Maria frowned. "We always have those during the busy months so—"

"We had a gentleman call early this morning, reserving us for the first two hours."

I felt my eyes widen as Maria stuttered, "The whole diner? For two hours? Whatever for?"

"Who the hell could even afford that?" Alice added, swiping her ID to scan in.

"I'm not sure. Based on the growing crowd, we think he's some bigwig celebrity on vacation."

We shuffled inside, and I quickly slid the latch behind us. Indeed, most of the people in the crowd were women, shielding their eyes against the sun and attempting to peek through the windows.

In the main dining room, the shades were still drawn, casting the usually bright space into a dull glow. A few men sat at the breakfast bar, chatting quietly or sipping on mugs of coffee. But my eyes gravitated to the back of the room, drawn by some unseen force which only seemed to multiply the longer I was here.

Sitting in the furthest booth, a lone man sat hunched over a newspaper. Save for a glass of water, the table before him was bare. His shock of white hair gleamed like the same shade of ice on the river's surface in late January. As if he could feel the weight of my stare, he lifted his head, eyes finding mine instantly.

Something instinctual curled low in my belly as the two of us held the others gaze. My mouth had gone dry, the sudden nerves coasting through my body freezing me to the spot. I hadn't a clue why; I didn't know this man, which made it all the more confusing as to why he looked equally as apprehensive of me.

Maria's voice seemed far away, Alice's hand on my shoulder nothing but a distant buzz. The man sat up straight, his mouth moving, but I couldn't hear a word he said over the rushing of my blood through my ears.

"Renita!" Maria's shout in my ear knocked me out of my trance and I jerked backwards, spinning to disappear through the kitchen door. I felt the rush of my power through my veins, the ache to release it, or to run.

"Ren you're scaring us." Alice's voice drifted over my shoulder gently, and I glanced to see her and Maria crowding the door. "I know he's hot, but you look like you're about to pass out."

"You know I'm not as shallow as that," I snapped before forcing a deep, centering breath into my lungs. Forcing the building typhoon of my magic to settle before I said, "That man in the booth is a Mer."

Renita

"Well, we're all Mer, actually."

Alice and Maria both jumped at the sound of the male voice at their back, before rooting themselves at my sides. He had trailed after us and now leaned in the doorway with his arms crossed. I fought the urge to gulp as I looked up at him, finding him much taller and imposing than he seemed from across the dining room.

His T-shirt clung to his lithe body, jeans sagging low on his hips. If not for his shock of white hair, he would have blended in with the other tourists perfectly. Up close, his grey eyes reflected the light of the room, shimmering like molten steel as they settled on me again. Something like an accusation burned in their depths.

"Though I don't understand how a simple Witch could tell that at first glance."

"She's anything but simple. Renita is renowned for her talent," Maria snapped, jumping in at my defense. I rested a hand on her shoulder as the man arched a brow, but didn't even glance her way.

"Is that so?" His look turned contemplative, head angling slightly as his gaze traversed down my body, then back up. I barely could breathe when his eyes locked on mine again, his intensity having not banked in the least. "And what is your specialty? I'd assume a beauty like you would serve well as an Empath."

I couldn't tell if he meant it as a compliment, or a way to demean me. Regardless, I ground my teeth together, letting the insults I wanted to hurl die on my tongue. I needed to focus, to shield myself in the most explainable way possible.

"I'm a Manipulative." It was the safest bubble to entrap my power, by allowing me the most range and variation. A Manipulative could change the color of the water or its temperature. Change a rivers track or an oceans tide. And if there happened to be a sudden flood to drown the arrogance out of the man before me, well, that was well within the range of a Manipulatives power too.

A slow smile spread across his features, revealing a dimple as he chuckled and again, I was struck speechless. Bitterly, I was forced to admit to myself that if I were crafted so

beautifully, I would probably wield some
arrogance too.

He had to be used to getting his way. And
with the way his eyes roamed me, he had to be
used to females frolicking to his bed from just a
glance. As if to highlight that intrusive thought,
there was a sudden burst of chatter as the
employee door swung open once again, before
swishing shut.

"Where is Renita?"

"Aunt Cora?" I was surprised to hear her
voice. "I thought you were away at council?" For
all the space he commanded, the male before us
was fully shoved to the side by my aunt who
barreled straight into the kitchen at the sound of
my voice.

"Yes, well," she grimaced up towards him
from beneath her gold-plated glasses, her look
scrutinizing. "That was the original agreement,
before they decided to arrive here unannounced."

"My guards were concerned we would be
refused extended hospitality." The male regarded
my aunt with similar scrutiny, the heat in his
eyes replaced by cool assessment. Cora stood
proud; her four foot nine inches having never held
her back this far. Stray grey hairs clung to her
amber curls, her brown eyes hardening when he
didn't back down.

"Guards?" I furrowed my brows, but my
question was ignored.

"If you think my sisters and I would be foolish enough to refuse a direct request, then you're more out of touch with your allies than you should be." The male chuckled again, my stomach fluttering at the warmth in the sound.

"I hardly expected an outright refusal." He lowered his voice, sliding his gaze back to mine. "The concern was for the unpredictable amount of time. Even I realize the delicacy of the request, which is why I wanted to make it in person."

"Which is appreciated but highly unnecessary and disruptive."

"Disruptive?" For the first time, something dark gleamed in his eyes. "I realize that it may have been audacious of me to show up like this. But you were paid a generous sum, and my men and I will do nothing to further to disrupt the water festival. I understand it is something your Coven holds dear."

Cora faltered for the first time, dipping her chin subtly in acknowledgment. Then she turned to me, easing me out from beneath Maria's protective death grip.

"You won't need to work today, Ren. I'd rather you save your energy for the water festival." I furrowed my brows, not understanding. She seemed to hesitate, then took a breath, her tone belying a sense of urgency that had me clinging to every word.

"Each of us Witches will be displaying our power as a show of good faith to the Sea King. As you are our strongest, I urge you to rest, and practice. Give him a show he'll never forget." Her grip urged me towards the door as she explained, but my mind was caught on the title she'd used.

"Sea King?"

"I'm better known as Cillian Maliah." The man before us stretched out a hand, and each of the women beside me bristled. "But yes, one day I will be the Sea King. If I'm not gutted in my sleep by the Sirens who seek to steal my throne."

I reached out, somehow keeping my fingers from shaking as I grasped his. His touch was warm and firm as we shook, fingers sliding off mine slowly as if he didn't want to let go.

"Renita," I responded, the urge to flee multiplying. The Sea King. The court responsible for my mother's death. The ones who would kill me I they ever found out—

"Even your name is marvelously stunning." The compliment speared me through the chest, and I looked away.

"Call me if you're overrun with guests today." My words were directed towards Cora, who took the opportunity to sweep an arm around my shoulders and finally move me out from under the impenetrable gaze of the Sea King. She marched me straight outside, shuffling us through the throng of women which had continued to grow.

A Mer King indeed. Only the most powerful of Mer could draw a human so naturally, almost similar to a Siren in that way. I felt eyes lingering on me as we left, my pull on them even stronger than his as my emotions whiplashed within me. I steadied my breath, feigning lightheadedness, and allowed Cora to lead me on the short walk home.

"Stay in the house Renita." The order was clipped in fear, and I nodded my head without argument. "I meant it when I told you to practice your craft. You will need to put on the performance of your life on Friday's Eve."

"I know." I did.

If I failed, I'd die.

Cillian was beyond audacious; he was a downright fool. I hadn't been in the water for days, as my precious willow cove was the perfect entry and exit to the water for the visiting Mer.

There were eight in total, six of which were Cillian's guards. More than once I caught them in the river with the tourists. My anxiety was palpable, but they just laughed it off.

Glamour, they claimed, could be used to blind the humans to their true forms. My concern was not with their security, but with my hidden treasure trove. I was excruciatingly aware of how close they came to finding it on their daily swims.

A piece of me wanted to ask questions, especially to the single red-tailed Mer. I was under the impression that they were some type of nobility as well, but everything I knew was second hand. I wanted to know why, and how, a member of a high-ranking family would be a guard, rather than living pompously. More so, I wanted to know why the true guards, each Manipulatives or Warriors by the looks of it, would be treated as equals by those of a higher rank.

The other half of me was a coward though and avoided the Mer like the plague. Though they kept their word, masking themselves as much as they could, it was impossible to completely erase the amount of magic hanging in the air of our little town now. With Cillian's added aura, we had even more tourists than normal, and Friday's water festival was wholly sold out.

The water festival. I couldn't tell if I dreaded its approach, or if I was craving to show off. He'd hurt my pride by assuming I could do no more than deeply feel and balance another's emotions simply because I had a pretty face. And Maria shooting her mouth off added extra pressure for my powers to show grandly yet remain controlled. I often felt physically torn between representing our Coven well, and prioritizing my own safety.

Each year, the water festival is held on July's full moon. The tourists who came were under the impression we had the technology and material to put on a genuine show, like they would see at their theme parks or gardens. Though we did, those mechanisms were mostly for show. The Witches were responsible for the majority of the effects and illusions, offering their power up to our Goddess, the night a symbolic ritual of the balance between power and life.

Every year, Cora and I were responsible for the grand finale. Colorful waves, bursts of spray, arching crests which glittered in the firelight. As a Siren, it was easy for me to wield that many effects at once. As an Empath, it was easy for her to help keep me under control. This year I would not have her strength to rely on.

With the Mer's constant presence on my riverbank, I was forced awake three hours before dawn to hike to the series of lakes dotting the mountainside above. I had to practice– had to perfect grasping each thread of control carefully. I wouldn't be able to go all out as I was used to. Cillian especially would be able to tell right away I was more than a Witch if I wielded too many formations at once. But paired with that, the grand finale couldn't be any less spectacular than normal.

"Damn it!" My palm slapped down on the water's surface, the shimmering cerulean fading against the ripples, and reddening with my agitation. I officially had just fourteen hours until the festival, and my formations were still progressing too rapidly to masquerade as a talented Witch.

"You're nearly as good as a Mer." I couldn't swallow my cry of surprise, which set off a flock of birds scattering into the dawn. I whirled around, naturally raising my arms, calling the water to crest around my shoulders, poised to launch and drown whoever snuck up on me. And when my eyes caught on him, I had never been more grateful for my ability to shift my tails appearance at will.

Cillian's eyes widened only a fraction, glancing between me and the gurgling wall at my back. Wordlessly, he pushed off the tree he was leaning against, striding straight for me.

Panic flared through me. He may not catch me with my tail out, but I was still in the water wielding magic I shouldn't have. And what makes matters worse is I did let myself stretch out earlier, needing a true swim after almost a week of being cooped up. And he just walked straight past my clothes, folded neatly on a rock at the edge of the bank.

"I didn't peg you for a skinny dipper." He flashed a wolfish smile, bare feet splashing at the lake's edge.

"What are you—" before I could even get the question out, he strode straight into the water. He stripped off his shirt with ease, tossing it behind him onto the ground without a care. His dress slacks, a smooth cream which complimented the rich tan of his skin, clung to the muscles in his thighs as he strode deeper to reach my side.

"Isn't something like this the cause of several burnings?" I swore there was a worried note below the tease.

Instantly, I let the wall of water drop, eyes scanning the forest's edge. He was right. The sun was beginning to stain the black sky back to blue, so the campers and hikers would be up soon. Reading my mind, he lowered his voice, adding, "My guards are the only other ones up here. Don't worry that pretty head of yours, mi tesoro."

His eyes were glued to me, and I shifted self-consciously. Though the dark mountain water lapped softly against my collarbones, I knew from the look on his face— and from the very fact that I had the same eyes meant for a life underwater— that he could see everything. And I was standing naked in a lake.

Rather than swimming further away from him, I found myself studying him as well, transfixed by the sight. Water droplets clung to his bangs and skin, tracking lazy routes down his well-built chest. He had twin tribal tattoos swirling down both of his ribs, arching over his hips to disappear beneath the waistline of his pants.

"I apologize." The statement came out slightly breathless, the restrained desire in his tone making him sound anything but apologetic. And his eyes, grey like a building storm, didn't leave me for a second.

"It's fine." It took more effort than it should have to turn away, my curtain of black hair dragging behind me as I made my delayed retreat from him. I ignored the sound of him following but startled when his hand suddenly snatched my wrist.

"Cillian!" I hissed, face flooding with a blush as he yanked me back towards him.

At this point I didn't give a damn if he were a God himself. No being would take my autonomy, simply because they thought they had the right. The instinct to shift and drag him to the depths became nearly unbearable, but the brush of scales against my bare legs had me instantly freezing.

No one knew the color of a royal Mer's tail. It was believed that they could alter the color at will or had other ways of disguising themselves. But as the sun finally crested the hills, bathing the lake in its warm glow, there was a flash of a thousand stars beneath the surface.

"My sincerest apologies." This time the desperation, and the faint pink stain on his own cheeks, had me believing him.

"I understand. I think." I forced a swallow. He gently turned me by the shoulders to face away from him, but I'd already seen far too clearly. My mind was a spinning mess, questions I couldn't ask piling up and threatening to erupt from me, but he spoke first.

"I usually have better control over it." His voice was tense, but his grip on me remained featherlight. There was the distinct rush and lull in the water from the steady pump of his tail, his unneeded effort to keep my head above the water. "I truly have no excuse. For some reason in your presence, I act without thinking. Without honor." My confusion multiples.

"You've only spoken to me twice. I think you're over analyzing your behavior." I tried to sound reassuring, but my racing nerves revealed otherwise. He released a rough laugh against my back, and I had to fight the urge to lean into him.

"Oh yes. When I cornered you in a kitchen to the point you nearly fainted. And in this moment, clasping you to me despite your visible discomfort, and state of undress." He heaved a sigh. "I'm aware of your aversion towards my presence, and yet I've disregarded that boundary continuously. Even going so far as to frequent your place of seclusion."

A spark lit in my belly as he admitted to using my willow cove on purpose. How dare he? The unnaturally heated looks were one thing, but he just outright admitted to being a pompous degenerate.

"I don't dislike you," I said, barely masking the gravel in my tone. Self-preservation continued to clasp at the waning strands of my self-control, and I quickly formed what I hoped was a meritable explanation.

"I don't have many positive experiences with the Mer. You're a very private, powerful and... complicated folk. And since you seem so bewildered by the notion, I'll plainly state that I don't have a taste for males who use their charm to mask their arrogance."

"So, you think I'm charming?" That damn chuckle reached my ears once again, but he released his grip on me. Rather than wholly pulling away though, his fingers skimmed down the length of my arms, as if he were savoring each second of the touch.

I'd experienced a male's desire before, on a few occasions. It was pleasant, but nothing compared to the roiling heat within me from the simple attentions Cillian has offered. It made no sense, and I feared it. This was a male who would sooner kill me than bed me. It seems there is far more than my magic that I would have to control until his departure.

"You may depart anytime you wish. My men will be sure to leave you your dignity. Please don't feel stuck in the water." There was a soft splash behind me, and I turned to see nothing but ripples on the surface. He had dove, leaving me to swim for the shore.

Mountain water was supposed to be cool. Refreshing. It was anything but. I was intimately aware of him somewhere below me, maybe watching, maybe following. Maybe ignoring my existence, I hoped. The water felt like smooth honey rolling over my suddenly aching muscles, and it left me scrambling on all fours up the bank.

My embarrassment didn't leave me as I quickly pulled on my sundress and boots, fleeing for the cover of the trees. As he said, his guards lined the path. None of them so much glanced in my direction as I hurried past. At the very least, it seems there was only one Mer I flashed. I sent another thankful prayer to the Goddess that I was blessed to control my tails appearance, and had remained poised enough to keep it from materializing. Unlike him.

My heart pounded harder than it ever had in my life as I raced down the mountainside. Not only was I a Siren surrounded by Mer, but now I had bigger problems. Whatever was simmering between us was obviously mutual to a certain degree, and that couldn't come to fruition. Especially not since his scales glittered with the same silver sheen as mine.

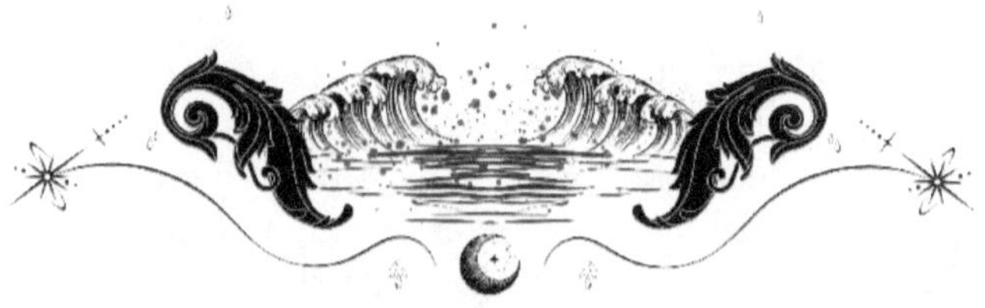

3

Cillian

Renita was a temptress. Yet despite the air she commanded, she somehow claimed a higher level of privacy than even the purest of priestesses. For a week I had barely gained more than a glimpse of her through the windows of her home, before trekking up that blasted mountain to… honestly, I don't know exactly what I was trying to do.

The Witches didn't need to convince me of her power. It was nearly as bright as their daylight, her aura emanating throughout the town even when she wasn't nearby. I'd never once witnessed a Witch with such power. The townspeople naturally gravitated to her, as did their guests, but what caught my attention was that my men were too.

That's why I thought her an Empath at first. For a Witch to draw the unconscious attention and emotions of a Mer… it was unheard of. If she'd noticed it, she hadn't let on. Other than her very apparent aggravation from the attention she'd been receiving from us.

I'd felt my curiosity growing over the days, but even before our exchange within the cool mountain lake it was clear that my fascination was uncontrollably blossoming into something more. More than once I'd snapped at my men, my irritation with myself boiling over inappropriately. And Alek was loving every minute of it.

He was my greatest friend, and pleasantry. But a noble for Goddess' sake, and with that came the affluence and ego that I must begrudgingly admit I share. Day after day I had to practically drag him from the river where he obnoxiously flaunted himself for her attention. And my men, though more wary, also couldn't seem to help themselves but purposely stray near her. This eventually led to us leaving the comfort of the ridiculously priced Air BNB my father had rented, and instead reside at the 3oo-year-old inn across town.

Part of me thought Renita wasn't aware of the reaches of her magic, but after seeking her out this morning, it was crystal clear she knew exactly what power she held. Her precision with the water was nearly flawless, as if they shared one body rather than her pulling at the threads of connection across the veil.

As a Manipulative she had the benefit of range with her power, but some of her movements reminded me of those my Warriors made. The two were by far the most similar in skill, but where a Manipulatives creation failed was in their mortality. Their strikes lacked the kiss of death, always pulling up at the last moment. A fantastic skill to use on the battlefield to distract and disorient, but never able to actually kill.

"She's stunning." Alek had fallen into step beside me at some point. I was so lost in my thoughts, and focused on not falling down this nightmarish mountain path, that I hadn't even heard him approach. I didn't bother to cling to my pride as I reached out to steady myself on the nearest tree trunk before casting a glare at him over my shoulder.

"She is a human and absolutely nothing more. The lot of you would do good to remember that." He snorted, rolling his onyx eyes with an extra amount of exasperation.

"Cillian you can't ignore the fact that she's a Witch. Sure, the pairing would be rather unorthodox, but she can easily live as long as you or I."

"A pairing? Are you insane?" I felt like the ground was slipping out from under me. Once I somehow skidded to a stop, panting, I sat right there in the dirt to catch my breath. Alek though was far from done and didn't seem inclined to let me interrupt.

"Am I supposed to pretend I didn't just watch what happened?" It was impossible to miss the tinge of jealously coating his words as he plopped beside me, instantly wiping his palms clean against his jeans and heaved a sigh.

"I merely point out the obvious. After avoiding you for a week, her presence makes you recklessly dive into unknown waters. And then of course there was that rather embarrassing lack of control over your own body—Oi!"

I cut off his words, jerking him towards me sharply. There wasn't a peep from my men as my mouth coasted over his, before shifting to the curve of his jaw. I pulled the collar of his shirt away, revealing the sun kissed russet of his skin, and began trailing my lips down the length of his neck. By now Alek's hand had raised to grasp the curls at the base of my neck, trying to jerk me away but I held fast, pressing one more open-mouthed kiss to the juncture of his neck and shoulder.

"You are the single luxury I allow myself to have," I murmur against his skin, fingertips playing with the ends of his long, sea blown locks. "I don't need another partner. Especially not at a time like this."

"You will be the King." His tone makes me pause, pulling back to find his eyes. A hint of desire lingered in the depths of his gaze, but not enough to stomp out the cool reality he was about to drown us under. "The day will come when you're expected to wed, and no one would say a word about a pairing with magic that visceral."

"Witch or no, I can't and won't have her." I lower my voice as I ease back, dropping my hands from him. "The land and the sea do not mix. Never have and never will. I will not ask a

stranger, especially not one who visibly despises
me, to abandon their Coven and their home.
Besides, she is not what we are here for, or have
you forgotten?"

As Alek drops his head, his expression
pinched and contrite, I rise to my feet and turn
slowly to face my men. Each sported a similar look
of remorse mixed with duty, and that was the only
thing which kept the steady swell of power from
growing within my aggravation even further. The
air shifted around us, seeming to crackle with the
voltage of my restraint.

"We are only here, because an entire
Kingdom wants me dead." I let my words strike
them, the gravity of the situation surpassing just
my life. "They seek to kill all royal Mer, which
includes some of your own kin. The Witches are
our last hope. I will not fumble gaining their aid,
especially since we have been anything but
forthcoming with our needs. Have I made myself
clear?"

There's a chorus of formal agreements and
apologies that I don't bother to address. Despite
the shift in my demeanor, I offer a hand to Alek
and help him to his feet before I continue down
the mountainside, faster this time. As soon as we
got back to the river, I was going in and sinking to
the bottom.

4

Renita

I hadn't been able to settle myself since this morning, and work offered no reprieve. Our little town had become so overrun with tourists for the festival that Aunt Cora had been forced to let me out from under house arrest, throw an apron on me, and hand feed me to the screeching wolves— also known as 14-year-old girls.

Six hours— and four spilled ice cream sundaes later— I was being lathered with the glittery body paint each dancer wore. Turns out, Bethany twisted her ankle last night and couldn't perform. And since this portion of the evening was Clarice's moment to shine, I was asked to fill in last minute.

"You don't have to be so nervous," she said, twisting my layers of dark hair away from my face to pin back. Her eyes found mine in the torchlight, the flames making the glitter on her face sparkle like stars.

That's one thing which made our water festival so unique. We did it the old way. For the duration of the event the power to the entire town was shut off, restored only after the grand finale.

Though this had become a way to fund our lives and offer a sort of security within the new world, the Coven strictly adhered to our own traditions. No matter how technologically advanced the world became, there would never be anything quite like connecting with the sacred Gods and Goddess' beneath the lights of flames and stars.

"I'm not nervous because of the dance," I muttered, and it was true. I could take each step and turn in my sleep, just like all the children raised here. "I'm just worried that after the day I had at work, it will sap me of the extra morsels of energy we all know I need to keep myself under control." Not to mention how nerve-wracking my accidental rendezvous at dawn with our guest of honor had been.

"Have faith," Clarice said, reassurance ebbing into the excitement in her voice. "The Goddess wouldn't have given you a day that would jeopardize you. You're walking proof that the universe has plans for us all, otherwise you would have never made it this far."

She finished pinning up my hair before holding up a mirror so I could see. Tiny diamonds shaped like water droplets arched over the crown

of my head, the pins holding back my thick curls
to fall over my shoulders in waves. Silver and blue
threads were woven between my dark locks,
which matched the many bangles adorning my
wrists and ankles. The dancers costume itself was
made of featherlight silk. It was stained black
against the body, but draped with a sheer,
shimmering fabric in various shades of blue and
teal which caught the air when I moved— similar
to the sway of aquatic plants.

I raised a hand to my painted face,
shocked by the detail Clarice was able to capture.
Silver scales dusted my forehead and cheekbones,
not nearly as brilliant as my own, but glimmered
in the firelight all the same. My lips were painted
a deep plum, complementing the warmth of my
skin tone, and the usual diamond stud beneath
my lower lip had been replaced with one of my
pale blue pearls.

"You look stunning, Renita. Nothing short
of it." I turned to see Cora staring at me, and she
held up a finger before I could protest. She
lowered her voice so that only we could hear.
"What gifts or curses you may have inherited do
nothing to change that."

I didn't have time to argue as the flutes in
front of the stage began to harmonize— our cue to
go. Clarice ran forward, excitement rolling off her
in waves as she took her place at the front of the
line. She was the Manta of this year's dance, the
deep navy's and dappled, flashing silvers of her
costume matching that of the sea creature. The
spirit of the Manta was always the forefront of the

dance, hoping to draw in good fortune and protection through the next year. I dared to believe it worked because at the very least, I had been protected here.

When the drums began, the dancers in line ahead of me glided out of view through the partition of smoke from the fires lining the river's edge and rose between us and the stage. I took a breath, schooled myself into an expression of neutral pleasantry, and arched my arms high as I stepped onto the glass floor. The stage, which had been erected earlier that day, was completely see through, which gave us the appearance of dancing atop the water.

I'd watched the dance from backstage and from the stands on the opposite bank many times, but there was nothing quite like participating in it. Magic gone wild, that's how Cora had described it to me as a child, and I'd clung to that description. It was the only one I'd found worthy. The air vibrated, taking its own breaths in synch with ours as we moved, dipping and leaping and spinning through the dark. The glitter on our skin flashed like falling stars in the firelight, the waves of our garments crashing like a stormy sea— and then a sudden calm.

The Manta rising, the tide pulsating slowly in and out in rhythm with the beats of its wings. The air around us had begun to glow a pure cerulean, the Manipulatives amongst us releasing the power into the water and lighting it up. The glass stage beneath us reflected the light, casting it upon the mountainside at our back as the voices of my sisters rose above the flutes.

Droplets in the air crystallized, before spiraling around us on the breeze. A controlled storm in slow motion, only made possible by the Empaths behind the stage feeding the dancing Manipulatives the emotions and energies they needed to not lose control. Or drain themselves. For this part, I didn't need such help.

Releasing a fraction of my control, the water beneath the stage began to roll and bubble, lapping softly at the glass pillars which weaved down into the river's muck. I heard the crowd gasp and knew the fruits of my power were beginning to be laid bare. I felt, rather than saw, the thin arches of water cresting above the stage. The river's heartbeat thundered alongside mine as I drew more water still, urging it to collect and swirl above us like a clock slowly ticking forward.

The Manta was circling me now, and our movements played off one another. Clarice and I side stepped each other in tandem, each bend and sway matching the others as the remaining dancers faded back to the edges, giving me just barely enough room to set up my own stage.

"Breath Renita." Clarice's voice barely met my ears before we were once again swarmed by the dancers. And I melted back, dipping off the edge of the stage to submerge beneath. Once the current dragged me beyond the fires I broke the surface, wet bangles jangling as I stripped them

from me as I centered my focus on what I had
been practicing to do.

The vortex of my power above the stage
had begun to pulse in time with the witch's power,
and a sense of starvation I usually kept buried
began to surface as I fed off it. Spirals of water
broke off from the pool, flashes of lilac and white,
blush and gold, the air rippling with tension as
they swayed and rose and burst like watery
fireworks. A wall began to rise behind the stage,
illuminated by the dancing firelight on shore. As
it pebbled with bubbling blooms of dripping
florals, droplets of rain fell in slow motion towards
the stage, each taking on its own color and hue.
That was when the thunder of applause
ricocheted off the river, and it was enough to
begin making my head spin.

My tongue was suddenly heavy, coated
thick with a need I've rarely felt. Though my skin
was running with sweat, my body was cold as it
continued curling and coiling through the dance,
and I felt my power begin to seep out of me at a
rampant pace.

Before I knew it, my own voice had joined
my sisters, the chorus of a Siren's song swirling
up into the dark night. A singular bolt of caution
flew through my nerves at the vague sense of my
scales prickling against my skin. My eyes flashed
to the stands, to the crowd on the far shore. If
they had been affected by my voice, it didn't show.
For now, it seemed the cacophony of my sister's
voices and power was enough to dilute the effect I
could have. And with that newfound reassurance,

I released my voice again, and this time was rewarded by an instant surge of bliss through my nervous system. I needed this. I needed this more than water and air combined.

My song mixed with theirs, deep as the ocean's caverns, smooth as her rolling surface. The grip on my control simultaneously grew stronger and wavered, my song making the watery show above us grow in magnitude and splendor. The heavens and the sea were waltzing above us, falling in sultry, dribbling paths, and shattering against the powerful crests breaking high from the river. Water became diamonds and night became neon, each atom electrified once in my grasp. This was it, one final push and then I could rest, hide… devour. It would be so easy, with an entire river at my disposal.

The curtain of water behind the stage suddenly shot skyward, piercing the swirling vortex. I thinned it out, pulling at each atom until they stood apart in a mist, crowning across the river and stage. And then it began spinning, faster and faster, shifting from navy, to teal, to green before dropping suddenly, crashing down into the riverbed and roaring over the stands.

The screams which reached my ears were louder than the applause moments before, jarring me out of my hungered state and I froze. Because the commotion wasn't louder than the rumble of sudden thunder. The flickering of the fires wasn't brighter than the electric shocks I watched dance between the atoms of my power still lingering in the air before me.

"Renita!" Cora's cry sounded frantic, but it was nothing compared to the immediate chill dousing all the heat and pleasure and pride from me at once. A singular thread of true lightning kissed the peak of the mountain above us.

"Renita, you must stop!" Cora was shrieking at me now, but I could barely hear her as the crackle of electricity filled the air.

"This isn't me," I whispered, knowing none of them could hear as a bolt of blue lightning struck the stage.

5

Renita

The mountain had come alive, rain and water and mud rushing for us in a sudden landslide. My feet were embedded in the river's edge. I refused to move as incantations and prayers and curses flew from my lips, my arms spreading wide as I solidified the rising water at my back into a thick wall of ice. All thoughts of self-preservation disappeared as my eyes zeroed in on the figures riding the muddy waves towards me. The figures singing like birds in the night.

Sirens. It had to be.

The humans were still screaming, but the witches had mostly gathered themselves. Pairs began materializing at my side, each Empath finding their Warrior, each Manipulative finding their Siphon, the bond between them a live wire as they called upon their magic to fight this sudden enemy.

Bullets of muddy water and gravel began raining down our heads. I called them all to me, not flinching as they impacted my skin hard enough to leave angry purple and black bruises. My sisters began to counterstrike, whips of rain and river water striking the Sirens off balance. Their scales and their shrieks, and the glare of the firelight off their pointed teeth, disappearing into the murky wall of death still speeding towards us.

I released my energy from the ice at my back, praying I had made it thick enough to absorb most of the impact as I recentered my energy. I didn't know if I could stop it. I didn't know how many Sirens had poured their energy into making it, but I could slow it. Weaken it.

With my feet still in the water, I fell forward, digging my fingers into the damp earth. I sucked in the air with as much force as I could, with the force needed for the ground to drink up as much of the rushing water as it could at a time. Every exhale was an evaporation, sending plumes of steam up into the air. It was working. The landslide heading for us was growing smaller, but it wasn't stopping. The Sirens swimming within it just drew what water I coaxed away back into their wicked attack.

The hair on my arms raised just seconds before the sizzle of electricity kissed the air. A single glance up had my heart dropping to the pit of my stomach as I locked on the violet flash of lightning bearing down on us.

"Move!" I screamed above the melody of a
rising Siren song. A single raise of my arms had
me siphoning my sister's magic away from them,
using it against them to push them back just far
enough before the bolt struck my wall of ice. I fell
forward, covering my head as shards of glass
rained down on me. The only shield between these
monsters and my home was now gone.

A rage I'd never felt before began to boil as
I stood. Eerily calm, I extended my hand, palm
down, fingers spread, parted my lips, breathed...

And then Cillian was by my side.

Gripped in his fist was a silver trident
which sparkled like sunlight on the sea, and his
free hand yanked me back behind him to place
himself directly in front of the wall of water
rushing for us. Then he spun the weapon so fast it
appeared to be a circlet, his precision taking my
breath away as he embedded the head of it into
the earth before him with a boom. The power
pulsing off him began pushing the wave of
rushing water back— and made me salivate.

"Use me." It took me a moment to realize
he spoke, my eyes finally finding his. And when
they did, I swear the world around us stopped.

They were supposed to be grey. They had
always been grey, like a north storm. So why were
they shining a shade of purple I knew intimately?

"Renita!" His shout knocked me back to
reality and I stumbled slightly, but his grip on me
didn't waver. "I'm a Siphon." His voice was raw,

desperate as he commanded, "Now by the Gods use me, or run."

I could have laughed. I could have cried. Of course, he thought we could be paired to play off one another's power, he a Siphon and I a Manipulative. Manipulative indeed. I was the wolf in sheep's clothing, and biting back a moan at the availability to Siphon the power off a willing Mer.

The tree line before us shredded beneath the weight of the landslide, obliterating any hesitation I had left. I leaned forwards against his back, my palm closing softly around the nape of his neck, and drank in the might of his power.

The effort to be careful could have killed me right there. Don't take too much, don't squeeze too hard, ignore the feel of your own sharpening teeth, while using your mixed powers to obliterate the attack. The other Mer were beside us now, Cillian's Warriors facing off with the Sirens who had stopped being cowardly and shot out from their murky hiding places. Their Empaths remained within arm's reach, the flashing knives in their hands swiping at the Sirens who got too close.

The Siphons and Manipulatives surrounded us, our group pouring our power into suppressing the wave. The earth groaned with the effort to sponge up the water we demanded it to, and the air dripped the excess of what we evaporated. The remainder of the landslide, a single cold, cutting wave crashed into us but the Mer didn't even budge.

My grip had shifted from Cillian's neck to
his shoulders, my nails biting sharp enough to
tear the fabric of his shirt. Once the water rolling
through us was swallowed by the river at our
backs, a heavy quiet settled over the night.
Though on the far shore we could still hear the
cries of the tourists, and of my sisters helping
them evacuate the scene, there was nothing on
our side except for the labored breath of the Mer.
And the overwhelming stench of blood.

There were three Sirens in total. The Mer
were dragging their bodies together in a heap,
speaking in hushed tones on what to do them.
Cillian's back beneath my palms was heaving for
breath, his shoulders flexing as he pulled his
trident from its place in the ground.

"Are you well, tesoro?" He murmured in a
half whisper, glancing over his shoulder to look
down at me. The grey of his eyes was still stained
at the edges with pale lilac, and I sucked in a
breath. My fingers reached up of their own accord,
resting lightly on his cheekbone. His pupils
dilated at the contact, but he didn't move.

"Color changing eyes, and Sirens after the
future Mer King." My voice was shaking but I
didn't care. "What aren't you telling us?"

He opened his mouth, but his eyes flashed
up to movement over my shoulder. I could hear
the thundering of someone running, and instantly
spun, taking several paces away as one of the
Mer, the noble if I'm remembering correctly threw
his arms around Cillian tugging him close. His

words were rushed and fumbling, and Cillian spoke in soothing tones. I could only watch, wide eyed as the Mer placed a kiss to his temple, and then his mouth, before releasing him.

"I feel less guilty for withholding, now that I know your Coven has kept its own secrets from me." The softness Cillian displayed moments before had shifted to something gruff and distrustful.

"Every Coven has secrets." Cora had materialized at my side, her hands firmly planted on my shoulders. Cillian didn't even look at her. With one arm wrapped around the waist of the noble, and the other propping the trident to stand high, his eyes dampened to black as he asked me,

"When were you going to reveal you were a Mer?"

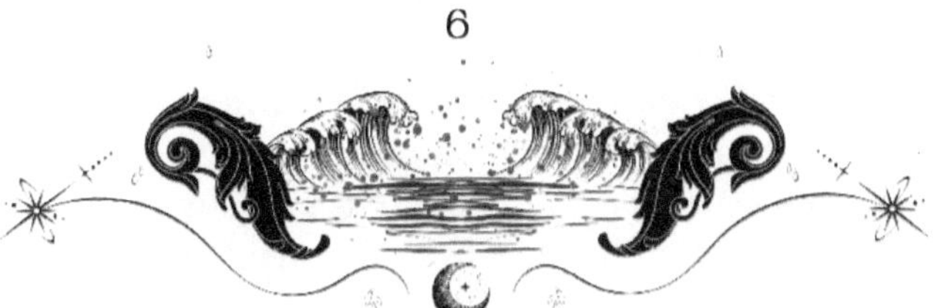

6

Cillian

"When were you going to reveal you were a Mer?" My grip on the trident tightened reflexively as I assessed her, and I was unable to ignore the flash of relief when there were no noticeable injuries besides a few bruises. I had been so blinded, so intrigued by her strength, that I didn't even consider the most obvious option.

Renita's eyes were blown wide, her lips parting in her shock, betraying the secret this town seemed to repetitively fail to keep. I hadn't paid any attention to the shops selling glittery mermaid items to the screeching children, tossing it up to the water festival and the magic coating the air. I should have paid it more heed.

Cora too had stiffened, probably trying to think of a way to play off what I'd just watched her do. What I'd just *felt* her do. Alek's presence was a force by my side, a mountain of power just waiting for my command. I held him back with a soft squeeze on his hip before stepping forward to lean over the pair of women before me.

"Don't bother denying it. I never met a Witch who had a treasure trove hidden in the belly of a body of water before." Renita's eyes flashed again at my words, but this time with a suppressed anger and I couldn't help but smirk. "Don't worry, mi tesoro. I didn't touch any of your precious jewels."

Mi tesoro my ass, she's been a bigger pain than anything. But I liked the way her body would tense with curiosity and annoyance when I used the endearment.

"We don't have a Mer among us," Cora said, and I finally looked at her. I forced the weight and coldness of an artic sea into my response.

"You're daring to lie to the Ocean King?"

"Future Ocean King..." Renita's words were hushed but they bit all the same, and I felt Alek stiffen at my back. She had regained her composure, eyes tracing me head to toe, and the glitter still clinging to her cheekbones just made the predatory gleam in her eye shine brighter. "You won't be the King if the Sirens kill you. Which I'm guessing is the true reason you're here."

I felt my lips curl into a grin seconds before leaning back and actually laughing. Her confusion was palpable, which I understood. I probably looked like a lunatic.

"As smart as she is beautiful. I'm not sure why I'm shocked." I turned, facing Alek. After a brief, wordless conversation, he easily plucked Renita out of Cora's grip. I watched with barely concealed amusement as he tossed her over his shoulder, ignored her sputtering curses, and dove into the water with her in tow. A single flick of his tail forced her fully under, and I waited with bated breath.

"What are you doing?" Cora's nails dug into my arm, and I quickly held up a hand so my men wouldn't grab her too.

"I know she's a Mer," I say, not taking my eyes off the place in the water where they disappeared. "I know she's a Manipulative. But I have yet to see her tail color." Which was blowing my mind considering I'd just had her naked in a lake that morning.

"She can't show you that!" The franticness in Cora's voice had my gaze shifting to her.

"Why?" I didn't hide my suspicion. If this Witch thought that she could fool me again—

"She was cursed. In her mind, by your own kind. But it was the Sirens who attacked her and her mother as a babe." Cora yanks on my arm harder. "That is why she lives with us here. She cannot survive in the sea if she's been cursed to a life without a tail."

I feel my jaw slacken as she explained, dots of white appearing at the edge of my vision. Could the Sirens actually do that? I'd rather die at their hands than suffer a fate so cruel. Before I could motion for one of my men to signal Alek, the belly of the river caved in on itself. I didn't need to move to see Renita, roughly ten feet below me. She was standing on the uneven, muddy river bottom with her hands balled into fists. With the lack of water Alek had been rendered useless, stuck laying with his ruby tail out in front of him.

I squat, tapping the head of my trident on a river stone to gain their attention, and both their heads jerk up at once. Renita is glaring with enough rage to spark a flame to life, but Alek is grinning like a man who just won the lottery.

"Well, it's rare to see you be beaten by an opponent," I said, sharing a grin with him. "Especially since you just took down a Siren. An uneducated Mer should have been easy."

"I told you she was strong," he protested, rolling his eyes dramatically.

"I am about out of all my fucking patience," Renita seethed, our laughter just serving to rile her up more. Somehow, her pissed off and cursing at me just made her even more attractive. Damn her. Damn her for lying. Damn her for making every part of this difficult, when it should have just been a smooth coalition with an existing ally.

A single snap of her fingers had the water caving in on them, and a second later a spout of it had Alek shooting out of the river to land on his ass beside me. I laughed again, before spreading my palm over his scales, allowing the Manipulatives in my rank to draw enough of my power to dry him off so he could shift back to legs.

Once done, he accepted the pair of sweatpants one of my men offered him and rose to his feet. It was difficult to ignore the few Witches joining Cora, their eyes suddenly locked on his physique.

A spark of jealousy went through me, which was immediately simmered out by a pulse of desire as Renita emerged from the water. Clean of mud and grime, her black curls clung tantalizingly to her curves. The costume she'd worn for the festival had barely covered her to begin with, and now soaked it left little to the imagination. I'd been respectful this morning, not looking even when everything in me screamed to devour the sight of her. That resolve shattered now as my eyes locked on her lips. Her wet, plump lips that her teeth were digging into in a rage so beautiful I could worship it.

She marched straight up to me, the water from the river writhing around her wrists and sharpening into a point which she unabashedly leveled at my neck. I blinked, surprised, before leaning into it, finding it sharper than I expected.

"Manipulatives cannot deal a killing blow, tesoro."

"No, but I can still make you bleed." Gods help me.

I swallowed and her eyes ever so briefly glanced to track the bob of my Adams apple. The tension between us throbbed, but then Alek gripped her wrist again, gentler than he did earlier, and she willingly dropped her arm.

"You led wild Sirens to my home." Her tone was anything but forgiving. "People could have died. Children could have drowned in front of you, and yet you expect us to save your skin?"

"Yes." She scoffed at my forwardness, rolling her eyes but I gripped her chin, forcing her gaze back to mine. Alek was stiff at her back, but I could feel his heated gaze skipping back and forth from me to her. I chuckled, and she stiffened as I let my curiosity get the best of me, if only for a moment. I rolled my thumb over her lower lip, savoring the way her head tilted in my grip, before resting it on the pearl beneath.

"I won't push into your business more than I already have." Immediately the tension ebbs from her body, and I make a note on how easy she is to calm if she's reassured.

"However," I added, not relinquishing my grip on her. "I now understand your distaste for the Mer, despite being one of us. Sirens are different, as you just saw. They're vicious and cruel and will stop at nothing to gain more power. I may not be able to return your tail to you, but together we can prevent others from suffering your fate."

Her gaze burned into mine for a moment longer before she pulled her chin away, and this time I let her go. Cora was by her side in an instant, throwing a towel around her shoulders and guiding her away. As the Witches retreated, my men began to regroup, began to discuss the best way to rid ourselves of the bodies still littering the river's edge before we ran out of time.

"Do you still intend to fight against what is so clear?" I couldn't meet Alek's gaze, but also didn't have the heart to lie to him about it further. This evening had made it painfully clear that I couldn't hide my inappropriate desire for her—but I could control myself. She was, after all, just another beautiful woman.

"You know," he said, running a hand over his wet hair, the gesture always betraying his stress. "For years I worried about our future. Yours mostly, but I don't think I'll have to for much longer."

"What makes you say that?" I ask, finding my voice, and the grin he's giving me makes both guilt and something darker flare to life in my gut.

"Well," Alek's brazen now, puffing his chest, eyes gleaming. I sense a building competition; possessiveness, that's what this is. "I'm also an unmarried noble. You're not the only male here fit for a woman like Renita."

"You're a horrible boyfriend for saying these things, you know that right?" He chuckled, pressing a kiss to my temple but it did nothing to alleviate the heat in my body. It's staining my face, rushing to my cock. Gods, this was going to kill me before the Sirens could even try.

Renita

Sleep did not find me gently. My emotions seemed to be in greater turmoil now submerged in the darkness.

Purple eyes.

His damn, lilac eyes. It had to be a coincidence. If it wasn't, I was unsure of what I would do.

Escape fate? Fight it? Take it.

For over a decade that shadowy figure in my dreams was a placeholder for comfort. That shade of color a calling. That energy intervening in my worst nightmares, regardless of my embarrassment or lack of control.

I slept fitfully, his arrogance and persistence chasing me farther than ever before. Did he even realize it? Goddess, let my dreams be one sided. Let him not realize I had been somehow finding him every night, welcoming him into my subconscious. I beg, let me hide.

"Renita."

I blink awake, my face hot from the lazy pane of sun cutting between the weeping boughs above me. When did I come outside? I couldn't be certain but didn't have the time to figure it out because I was asleep half in the water with one of the Mer staring down at me.

I choked back the scream in my throat as I scrambled to my feet, my wet hair whipping me in the face. The Mer didn't bother hiding his grin, clearly humored by my hyper reaction.

"What do you want?" I snapped, dragging my fingers through my hair to rid it of any grass or leaves, and focused on calming myself.

"To introduce myself properly after mock-drowning you." I felt my eyebrow tick skyward as I studied him. The noble who planted a kiss on the future King's mouth.

His waves of dark hair were newly braided and bound atop his head. I'd gotten a good look at his tail last night, a luscious ruby red, and though he was properly clothed today his powerful muscles were still evident. He shot his hand out, palm finding mine before I could even process words. "My names Aleki Kauahi. Known to the court as the Red Tide, the pride of the King's guard."

"Are you so esteemed because of your strength, or because of your special relationship with the future King?" The question had left my mouth before I could think better of it. His eyes widened only slightly, before a boom of warm laughter drowned the awkward silence between us.

"My strength," he finally said, thumb caressing the back of my hand before he released me. "Though I'd be a liar if I said it didn't play a part in establishing that relationship."

"I don't understand why you've come to see me, so please excuse me. There are many things I need to help take care of," I say, turning away and marching towards the house.

My mind had shifted, becoming a whirling mess as the reality of what happened last night dawned on me. We had bodies to dispose of— tourists who were probably hurt or traumatized and would surely sue. I couldn't imagine the number of cops which had probably gathered upriver at the event stage. And the magic community? My Gods, my poor Aunt was probably stressed down to her very atoms.

"Dampen your worries, Cillian has handled everything." Aleki's voice is light, upbeat even, as he trots along beside me. I could have laughed if I weren't so stressed, watching this mountain of a man glue himself to my hip like a frolicking puppy.

"Your future King could not have possibly—"

"Our, future King," Aleki interrupted me, a sudden serious edge in his voice. "He has taken care of all of it. For you, I might add." I stopped dead in my tracks, fast enough to make Aleki skid a little.

"You expect me to believe he has not only swindled the tourists, but the humans mass media and law enforcement as well?" My words were clipped but he just beamed at me.

"He even personally addressed the head of two other Covens just a few hours ago. Explaining the cause and blame of this attack, ensuring it falls squarely on our shoulders and isn't shifted to your Coven."

The willow branches were the only sound, shushing against one another in the light summer breeze. That and the pounding of my heart in my chest. The cool wash of fear, accompanied by... want. I ignore it, that reaction could only be because now I feel indebted to the bastard.

"That was..." I swallowed, unable to meet Aleki's eyes.

"The least he could do," Aleki said, the words buzzing against my skin not quite right. While I agreed, I had also thought it was kind. I raised a palm to my forehead, shutting my eyes, taking a breath. When I opened them again, I noticed Aleki had crowded me slightly.

I bristle, tilting my head back the extra few millimeters I need now to study his face. His broad shoulders sliced through the daylight, casting a shadow over the lower half of my body. His eyes are inquisitive, but I don't miss the buried shimmer of interest and that's what keeps me quiet.

I'd never been with a Mer. Never been with anyone besides an occasional tourist here or there to satiate myself. But never someone I knew, never someone I had any type of connection with. And I could certainly do worse. I hadn't missed the way my sisters ogled Aleki last night, the toned planes of his bronzed skin impressing even me through my rage. The air shifted again bringing his scent to my nose. Salt and coconut, and something tangy.

"I believe Cillian's actions were noble." My voice was a whisper, the words my only excuse to cling to as I took a step back. "Though I believe he acted out of necessity and obligation, I can realize that he is a person of sincerity. I know he didn't mean to bring danger here."

"Ahhh, mi tesoro. Sweet words coming from you are a luxury indeed."

Despite the humidity clinging to the air, goosebumps littered my skin as I whipped around at the sound of Cillian's voice. He was seated in the grass, back braced to the cracked wood of the willow and sunning himself like a damn cat. His pure white hair seemed to be tinged with dirt, the dark greys of his eyes a hazy mix of amusement and exhaustion. By the looks of it he's been there for hours, and I felt my skin flushing as I realized he had probably sat there the whole time I'd napped outside.

"You perv—"

"Oh, there it is, thank the Gods," he said, chuckling as he cut me off. His eyes were warm when they met mine, a smug grin on his face. "Careful, because you were beginning to sound like you don't entirely detest me."

The urge to bite him, to wipe that damn smile off his irritatingly handsome face, multiplied. I scoffed, the sound sharp and aggravated, turning on my heel and doing my best to not bolt for the safety of my house.

8

Renita

"With‑holding political secrets is inexcusable! I don't care if we have an alliance. Your actions have unnecessarily put my people's lives at risk!" Whatever shred of gratefulness I'd felt towards Cillian's actions, aunt Cora did not reflect.

I'd only seen her this outraged once before, shortly after my arrival. The Coven Leaders in Salem had expressed concerns about my heritage, to which she nearly drowned them all out of their old mansions and passageways. The reaction had nearly cost her her magic, which is what caused me to now stand and place my hands on her shoulders, smoothing down her prickling rage.

"It was not my intention to keep it from you." Cillian's voice was serene. "I simply wished to not distract you from your water festival, as I understand it's a sacred practice to you."

He was back to his obnoxiously clean-cut self. Gone was the bedraggled hunk leaning against the tree, replaced by a glasses wearing three-pieced-suit businessman lounging at the breakfast bar in the diner. Aleki, always by his side, had also cleaned up, yet his pressed jeans and sports coat were far more demure than his boyfriends. Aunt Cora and I stood on the opposite side of the counter, and I coaxed the coffee pot out of her hand before she shook it so hard it shattered.

"Calm down mom," Clarice piped up from the end of the counter. She flipped through a magazine lazily, clearly eavesdropping. "They literally handled everything and even smoothed over the news leak. There was no way we would have been able to convince the press that it was just a landslide without them…" she trailed off, nails curling the page in her hand.

"Without them glamouring the humans." Cillian's eyes met mine, heating ever so slightly. I raised my glass, taking a sip before mumbling, "Brainwashing them is a better word actually."

"You paint me so cruel." He pressed a hand to his heart, and I audibly groaned, rolling my eyes.

"I'm gonna be the one that outright says it." Aleki spoke up, interrupting whatever whining complaint Cillian was prepping to toss my way. He leaned back on his stool, scratching the back of his neck.

It struck me how stressed he was. To this point, I'd only seen him as a haughty noble, or the playmate of the future King. But he was a Warrior too, and a part of the King's guard. If he had nightmares like mine, last night was probably a hellish version of them. I felt a pang of guilt for the first time as he leaned forward, resting his elbows on the bar to look at me at eye level.

"They're going to keep chasing him. Keep trying to kill him." His throat bobbed. "We have no idea how many of them there are. We have records of the ones banished, but those date back centuries. There's no way to know if they're even still alive."

"Or, if they have found one another, developed their own attempt at a community, and procreated." Another one of the guards spoke, with so much ice in his tone it had my nerves spring to life. I refused to allow the shudder within me to surface as he added, "We shouldn't have ever let any of the beasts live."

"This just further pushes me to insist you leave." The anger in Cora's voice had ebbed slightly. "I understand we have an alliance to aid, but last night we were unprepared. You've shattered the trust our people have built over the centuries, and because of that I will not risk my Coven. You'll have to seek help elsewhere."

Clarice and I whipped out heads towards her at the same time. My lips were parted, but nothing came out. Fortunately, Clarice was already shouting.

"Mom, they'll kill him!" She was off her
stool, stomping around the coffee bar to our sides.
"There was only three of them and they nearly
killed everyone here. Hundreds of witches and
nearly a dozen Mer! If not for Renita risking
herself by letting loose, we would all be dead!"

I felt their eyes on me then, Aleki and
Cillian. Blood pounded in my ears, drowning out
the sounds of my families bickering as I turned
away, trying to count my breaths.

"And he's only a Siphon for goddess' sake!"
Clarice was not one to be subdued, her fist
pounding the countertop. "If we send him away
and his Warriors die protecting him then he's a
sitting goose!"

"I beg your pardon?" Cillian looked
outright offended, and Aleki stood from his seat,
the need to defend his King and his partner
overriding his self-control. The marble countertop
cracked under his palms, just sending my aunt
into another uproar.

As the three argued, my breaths grew
more erratic. I felt the creeping sensation of power
up my spine, a buzzing of static on my fingertips. I
began to salivate as the same taste of power and
need that I'd felt during the water festival
reawakened in me.

Chaos. Fear. Anger.

Calm.

I blinked, suddenly in shadow, suddenly warm even though the chill in my bones had made me feel like I was going to pass out.

"It's just an anxiety attack, tesoro." Cillian's gentle voice cradled my emotions while his arms coaxed me to him. My hand on his chest, feeling it rise and fall, his hand on mine in gentle encouragement to match pace.

His eyes flared to violet briefly, but he held my gaze, held me together on the verge of falling apart. Slowly, the allure of chaos faded. The desire on my tongue banked to an amount I could swallow down. Breathing was easy, though a sense of numbness had settled in my bones.

"I will go." I said it so quietly I thought no one had heard, but when I turned my gaze from him, I found the others staring at us.

"Renita." Cora's voice pitched with panic, reaching for me but I recoiled. The thump of Cillian's heartbeat against my palm, ticking slightly faster after my words, sent tingles through my body.

"I am a Mer, tail or not." Cora clamped her mouth shut as I found my resolve, using her own lie to douse any argument.

"They're trying to kill my future King, and the power I drew from him last night was... insurmountable. Irreplaceable. I highly suspect that's why none of your Manipulatives dared to even try to use it, as it would overwhelm them.

And Aleki, strong as he is, isn't a good pair based on his given magic."

"It's suicide." Cora actually glares at me, and I understand her deeper meaning. She knows I wouldn't be harmed by the Sirens; it's the Mer who would kill me if they found out what I truly was. I raise a brow, unable to resist my nature and rise to her challenge.

"So, you're admitting you'd be sending him to die?" I take a step towards her finally, gripping her outstretched hands. "I can help them. Maybe even myself. We both knew I could only remain hidden away here for so long, that the Ocean would eventually find me. Let it be on my terms." The words were both so cryptic and so pure.

"You would do this willingly?" Cillian sounded taken aback, humbled even. Cora's hands squeezed mine even harder, nails threatening to draw blood. Without breaking eye contact with her, I nodded my head.

"You may be to blame for endangering my home," I said, feeling Clarice wrap an arm around my shoulder. "But you and your men are the only reason we are still standing here in one piece. I owe you as much."

"I do not wish for you to endanger yourself further simply because of a debt," he snapped, shocking us both. Annoyance prickled along my shoulders, and I turned to level a heavy look on him, daring him to challenge me further.

He was glaring at me, or trying to. If anything, he looked like he was internally squirming. I felt my lips curl, changing tactics.

"Would you rather I not join you?" I asked, tilting my head just slightly, letting the heady sense of glamour fill my voice freely for the first time in my life. His eyes blew wide, body stiffening for half a second. Behind me, I could feel the weight of Aleki's gaze. Two Mer hooked with just one sentence. I grinned. "That's what I thought, but thank you for clarifying."

Cillian's gaze flew between Aleki and I, before he spun and disappeared out the door without another word. Aleki let out a low laugh, hand dropping on my shoulder as he passed by to follow.

"We'll see you on the mountain path then, little predator." His touch slid just a tad lower on my arm, the heat from his body palpable before he released me and left.

"Okaaay." Clarice wiggled her brows at me, but I shook my head at the same time Cora snapped at her to hush.

"Renita, you've realized what you've done? You'll be alone with the very people who already tried to kill you once."

"I—"

"I already lost your mother," she cut me off, yanking her to me in a hug with a force a woman of her size shouldn't be capable of. "Do not force me to endure the agony of losing you too."

"I promise," I whisper into her hair, pulling Clarice to me as well. I would be fine; I couldn't be anything less. I would only need to suppress what I was for a little longer, for just as long as it took to help alleviate the threat over his head and return home. Then we would be safe from my world forever. Because if I saved the Ocean King, I saved us all.

9

Cillian

It had rained overnight, so the morning breeze curling over the mountain above us was for once cool. Being raised in the Artic Sea, I often found the heat difficult to deal with, and knew I was swiftly approaching my endurances limit.

The Witches had provided us with far more than we deserved. Credit cards. Enchanted blades. Waterproof clothing to help mitigate any accidental shifts— my men didn't have the same ability to hold a human form like I could once wet. It would only take one inch of too much water, and they'd be a bunch of flopping fish on the ground until I could intervene.

Renita had joined us wordlessly, her eyes dark like the ocean's depths. She was avoiding my gaze, rather watching my men soak in the lake before the long trek ahead of us.

The plan was to hide on the mountain path until we reached the Susquehanna River. I was fairly certain the rogue group of Sirens who attacked us here would not be followed. It was one thing for the future King to be visiting a Coven on land, but it would be unheard of for him to not immediately return to the sea. I was hoping, as difficult as this journey would be, that the unorthodox nature of the plan would protect us. Alek wanted to fly rather than walk, prioritizing time, but after the Sirens attack on an entire town because of me… well, I didn't want to add a plane crash onto my list of sins.

"The mountains are as old as we are." Renita's voice startled me out of my thoughts, and I shifted my gaze back to her. Her thumb and forefinger played with her pearl labret, purple today, as the only sign of her unease. "It won't only be the Sirens hunting us in these woods. Especially at night. I seriously wish you would consider driving."

I couldn't silence my groan of disdain, my stomach giving an instant flip. Driving would take days or weeks. The bumps and the curves of the road being something none of us would stomach well.

"We would only be able to be on the road for a few hours at a time, if that," I said with a sigh. "We aren't built for such things."

"You also aren't built to deal with cryptids and fae." Her answer was instantaneous, and heated, making my nerves roll for a whole other reason. I felt the corner of my mouth twitch, and knew I was smirking when I saw that familiar spark of annoyance in her eyes.

"Don't tell me you're worried for me now." She grits her teeth, but I'd gotten the result I

wanted, watching the faintest blush stain her
high cheekbones as she averted her gaze.

"The whole point is to keep you alive and
yet you're making the dumbest decisions
possible," she grumbled.

"You're blushing even without me
glamouring you." I ignored her statement, leaning
slightly closer. "So apparently I'm doing
something right."

Someone behind me cleared their throat,
and I swallowed the instant growl of annoyance I
felt building in my chest. Turning, I see Alek
smirking at me like a jackass. I bite my tongue,
leaning away from her and crossing my arms, not
giving him the satisfaction of seeing me
embarrassed.

"Well, if the two of you are ready to get on
with it," he gestures to the rest of the group
behind him, freshly dried and tying the laces of
their new hiking boots.

"You'll be following me." Our gazes snap to
her, but she rolls her eyes. "Oh, please don't look
so offended. We all know your sea legs don't know
where to step on uneven terrain. Not to mention
I'm the only one here who knows how to spot a
supernatural booby trap between the shadows of
the leaves."

With that she marched away, her open
rain jacket billowing around her like a cape as she
strode past my men. I forced a nod to follow her,

remaining still as they paired together and began to shuffle off.

"Captivating and commanding." Alek breaths the words I dare not utter. "Fit for a King indeed."

"We don't choose these things." My voice was harsher than I intended, but I couldn't hold my aggravation back. "I do not have that luxury. The Goddess has bestowed a plentiful amount of royal Mer for me to have my choice of when I feel the time is right. This woman is not one of them."

"Meh, you'll never be convinced of that." Alek slides his hands into his pockets, nudging me forward with his elbow so we actually begin to follow the others.

"I don't have to be convinced to choose," I growled, my fingers twitching before curling into fists.

"You misunderstood me." Alek's teasing had banked, softening into something more serious. I didn't look at him, just followed his gaze to where she led us, her raven locks whipping in the growing wind. As if summoned, she glanced over her shoulder, her gaze finding mine briefly before flicking to Alek, and then turning back around. He released a warm chuckle, hand sliding down to mine to intwine our fingers.

"You'll never truly be able to let this go, unless she tells you what color her tail was."

10

Renita

The Mer were less helpless than I thought, but they still had no sense of awareness. More than once, I had kept one of them from killing themselves just by doing something stupid like walking off a cliff because they were following the sound of a bird, or breaking a leg because they were watching the sun set rather than watching their footing.

And they were fascinated to learn. Night after night around the campfires I was endlessly peppered with questions until they drifted off like tired puppies. Over the course of a week, I'd learned their names, their powers, and got used to their vivid personalities.

Leonardo, an Empath, was a brute with the others, but always made sure everyone's water bottles were filled and that they weren't in the sun too long. Paired with him was the Warrior Nyx, a quiet man who shared very little.

Then there were the twins, Juan and Mateo, who seemed to take it upon themselves to become my personal bodyguards. They were raised in a matriarchal household and beheld me with the same respect as they did their future King. Sylus, an English Mer, was the yappiest of them all, and his poor Warrior companion Maximus was doing his best to reel him in and give me some reprieve.

Cillian had remained oddly stoic and distant, making my nerves stir occasionally. He probably realized I wasn't going to fall for his charms and sleep with him, so just moved on from the notion. Aleki however seemed intent on the opposite track.

More than once, he had stepped in to 'assist' me with climbing over a fallen log or scaling a rock face. The Appalachian trail was a weaving woodland of many obstacles, which I felt I was faring fine with, but despite their struggles the Mer noticed. And I hated it.

I also hated how his gallantry made me feel warm inside. It wasn't that I was neglected through my life. The Coven was full of supportive men and women who never failed to make me feel at home. And normal. But... it lacked the gentle attentions.

The Witches all knew what force of nature I was, only stepping in during times of emotional distress. Now, to have people noticing a struggle and helping without the slightest air of judgement... it was chipping away at a buried place inside of me. I could feel roots beginning to grow with each gentle check-in from Mateo. Each dictated water break from Leonardo. Each time Aleki gripped my hips to steady me, his fingers lingering half a second longer than necessary. By the end of the first week, I'd felt my hackles lower, and for some reason felt more relief than fear.

Now I sat at the edge of a gently running stream, something that would go away once the runoff from yesterday's thunderstorm evaporated. The Mer were still secluded away in their waterproof tents, waiting till the sun rose a little higher before they risked stepping out into the damp world.

I breathed it in, the mud, the wet grass, the stone. Each scent was distinct, if you focused well enough. My left shoulder was wet from the dripping leaves above me, my right fingers hovering over the few centimeters of water at my disposal. I hadn't shifted since the morning before the water festival, and I'd never felt so dry and tight in my own skin.

My fingernails elongated into points as they dipped in, a shudder running through me. The back of my hands became glassy, microscopic scales reflecting the morning light. I was holding my breath so I wouldn't start panting. Or crying.

"It must be difficult." A warm hand settled on my shoulder, steadying me as I startled. Aleki's voice was warm on my skin as he squats down next to me, peering down at my shaking hands.

I'm frozen in equal parts shock and fear. The scales on my hands hold no color, reflecting only what is around us, but I don't know what any of it means in the context of an actual Mer taking it in. Would the clawed tips of my fingers give me away? Would the fact that there were scales even though I apparently didn't have a tail be the proof of what I was?

Aleki though seemed perfectly unbothered. His warm hand slid down my arm to spread across my fingers, curiously exploring their sharpened tips. "It figures you would reflect the physicality's of a predator," he muses, chuckling lightly.

"What do you mean?" I wasn't feigning my ignorance. My mother, in the years I had her, never spoke about my scales other than the importance of hiding them. Their color would attract danger.

"Depending on your lineage, and what the Goddess' intends for you, a Mer's features will represent certain aspects of the world around them. Take me for example." He still hadn't released my hand, his large fingers slipping between mine, caressing the skin in slow, fluid strokes.

"I was blessed to have a red tail, but my markings reflect that of a tiger shark." He grinned widely, and I finally noticed the slight points to his teeth. "I too have predatory aspects, indicating my strength and hunting styles. As well as the characteristics of the magic I would have with my Warrior abilities."

"Hunting styles?" It seemed all I could do was ask questions now, the rest of my energy focused on not allowing my heart to leap into my throat as his fingers graced the pulse point on my wrist, squeezing gently.

"Well of course." A half smirk ticked the corner of his mouth. "Warriors have jobs beyond the battlefield. We hunt together, providing food for the community." His voice lowered just slightly, his breath ghosting against my neck as he added, "And it makes taking a mate particularly exciting."

I felt my lips part as I turned to look at him, felt a lance of heat trickle down my spine as his gaze dropped to my mouth, and returned to mine more heated. Before I could move, a sudden gust of mountain wind threw my hair into my face, and the tinkling song of pixies shattered the silence of the morning.

"Shit!" I was upright in a second, running the short distance back to the camp. There were several shouts of surprise, one of my own when I saw Leonardo swinging one of the enchanted blades for one of the small Fae chewing the top of his tent.

"Are you insane!?" I caught his wrist with more force than I intended, watching his eyes widen in surprise as I disarmed him within the blink of an eye.

"A single drop of blood and these little piranhas will go into a feeding frenzy," I chastised sharply, catching one of the pests by its foot before it could tangle itself in my hair. "Our skin and scales will become their breakfast, especially if you kill one of their own."

"Well how was I supposed to know?" Leonardo was glaring at me now, but his gaze was more calculated, no doubt trying to figure out how a woman of my size was able to overpower him with ease.

"Regardless," I huffed, turning from him and searching the area of woods around us to find anything which could aid us. "Choosing murder first just gives another qualifiable reason as to why I hid what I am from you. Why would I want to be a part of a vicious civilization who holds no value over any life but their own?"

The grumbled insult was meant to deviate him, distract him from my intervention. I stalked a few feet away, feeling their curious eyes on me as I used the blade to slice a couple of branches of raspberries from their perch. After yanking my pack from my private tent, I sat cross legged and pulled out my motor and pistol, a bag of salt, and bottle of iron tablets.

"What are you doing?" It was Cillian's voice but all of them were crowding me, trying to get a glimpse of me crushing and mixing the berries with the other materials.

"Would you rather they eat us?" I countered, pausing to peer up at him with an arched brow. Only he would walk the Appalachian Trail in designer jeans.

"You intend to... feed them?" He asked, confusion lacing the question. He still looked half asleep, his stormy eyes hazy, but there was more curiosity there than apprehension. I softened the edge to my voice, shrugging.

"Well, they're hungry." The hoard had move on to the tent's bright orange ropes, chewing on them with shrill buzzes of disdain at the taste. A minute longer and I was scooping the mixture out in my palm, releasing little clicks with my tongue to get the pixies attention.

I felt the Mer back away as the creatures swarmed me, tickling me with their metallic wings, their little pink bodies scuttling over my arms and legs to get at the food. It made me giggle, but I held my arm steady as they ate.

"It has the sweet scent and texture they're looking for," I offered. "And the added iron will satiate their bloodlust enough to not take my fingers off." I hesitated for a second, before glancing at Cillian again. "You wanna feed one, Prince?"

Surprisingly, a smile took over his face. He was seated by my side in an instant, his palm held out expectantly. I felt myself returning the smile and painted his fingertips with some of the berry mixture. Three of the pixies still fighting their way to my hand immediately ventured to the new source of food.

"If they do start to nibble, just lift them off and they'll fly away," I warned gently. "Please don't be stupid and wait for them to draw blood."

"Settle your concerns, tesoro." He didn't even look at me, grinning like a kid as he reached for more of the berry mix, drawing more pixies to him.

Aleki had at some point lowered to my other side. Earlier passions forgotten, he too excitedly scooped up some of the mixture, talking gently to the pixies which flocked him. Slowly, each of the Mer did the same, until we were sitting in a ring in the woods, feeding pixies in comfortable silence. Even Leonardo seemed to be experiencing his idea of a smile.

Once the pixies had eaten their full, they fell asleep in little pink piles beneath the wildflowers at the trails edge. Their bulbous bellies took on the appearance of fat capped mushrooms, their glamour not powerful enough to fool me, but enough for the humans and animals to leave them be while they slept.

"That was... something." Cillian was by my side again, offering me a kerchief for my hand which I took.

"You'd get to experience many wonderful things, if you didn't just attack what you don't understand," I replied, not meeting his gaze.

I felt awkward now and hoped I didn't show it. To be honest, I didn't know what to think of him, or Aleki for that matter. They practically made out right in front of me, but then shamelessly flirted as if I was the only creature in their sites. It should sicken me.

"I can practically hear the gears in your brain turning Renita." My eyes cut back to his, and I wish they didn't. Violet danced at the edges of his irises, an undistilled heat in his voice as he added, "Care to share?'

"No." I turned my back on him and began to break down my tent. When he moved closer to help, I slapped his hands away. "I said no." My voice had gone darker, something in my expression being enough to make the smile fall from his face. Maximus appeared over his shoulder, gaze shifting from me to Cillian.

"Allow me to assist you, my King." Cillian's jaw was set with clear frustration, and maybe a little pain, before his gaze iced over.

"Very well."

The forest had awakened around us now, the buzzing of bugs beneath the chorus of birdsong. Faint cracks and pops of the trees shifting and of small animals scurrying across the dirt floor. Everything seemed to echo, pounding in my skull as I worked in silence to break down my tent.

I jumped when Nyx appeared at my side, but the Mer just nodded and took my tent bag from me. After securing it to his pack with two clips he just walked away.

"Wait…" I stepped to follow him but was cut off by Juan and Mateo.

"We wait for your lead, Miss Renita," Juan said, slipping my pack from my shoulders and handing it off to Mateo.

"What in the world—"

"You just saved our lives." This time it was Leonardo, who huffed an annoyed breath. "We were already in your debt, as you left your Coven to protect our King."

"And now you are in our charge." Cillian's purr reached my ears as he strode over, sliding a pair of sunglasses onto his face and offered me his arm. "Prepare to be treated like royalty, Renita Lenox."

Fire and ice ran side by side through my veins as he flashed me a shit eating grin. How he figured out my last name I wasn't sure, but that was one step closer to discovering the secret my mother died to keep.

I steeled myself, straightening my shoulders, raising my head, and marched straight past him without another word.

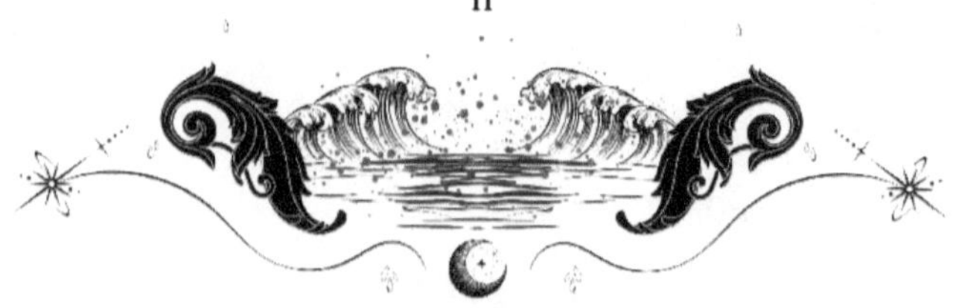

11

Cillian

I reveled in the way she squirmed from the new attention. It's difficult to explain really, why pissing her off turned me on so much. I guess it was just me getting back at her for how jealous she'd made me by just simply existing.

Alek too. I tried to ease the bristles of jealousy, the flashes of pain. It wasn't like I was threatened by his interest in her. I knew that a single word from me would end it right there, even if it was selfishly to pursue her without his competition. But I didn't, because I was curious as to how far she would entertain this. Us. And the bastard knew it so pushed her even more.

He knew full well I was awake and watching his little rendezvous with Renita this morning, dragging his hands all over her while lifting his gaze to meet my glare. And Goddess, her reactions were beautiful. I'd be a liar if I said it didn't cross my mind in the past days— what it would be like to have them both. Alek's weight against my back, Renita's legs around my hips— damn it, I was already hard again.

Sylus was the only one bold enough to verbalize his opinion on our very obvious intentions now. He sidled up to me during lunch, made casual conversations about more than one member of her Coven, before moving onto Renita herself. I damn near broke my oath and siphoned away his full magical capabilities, when he asked her if she found him interesting enough to pursue, what my opinion on their union would be. Through gritted teeth I shared how she didn't strike me as a woman who would chase him the way his ego would require.

Mateo and Juan became even more obnoxious, hovering over her throughout the day. I was their future King for Goddess' sake, but they still wouldn't let me get within arm's reach of her. At one point Mateo physically intercepted me before I could walk beside her, slinging an arm around my shoulders and holding me back.

By the time we made camp that night I was ready to fist fight my own men, but the sight before us had me pause. Now, I couldn't tell you how far we've walked or what state we were in, but the glassy mountain lake in front of us was so beautiful I didn't care.

Maximus and Sylus had already stripped down, closely followed by Leonardo and Nyx. The group dove into the water with relieved cries, sending frothy waves to break against the shore as they finally could shift for the first time in days. Alek was stripping down now too, but I paused before following him, eyes searching the trail behind me.

Renita sat with her back pressed against a tree trunk, hugging her legs to her chest and resting her chin on her knees. She was looking at the water with such longing that it shattered the excitement I felt. Mateo and Juan flanked her, more like her guards than mine, so I didn't even try to approach. That said, I was willing to take my time, give her a show if she wanted it.

Alek's mouth twitched into a knowing grin as I undid the buttons on my shirt, discarding it on a nearby rock before squatting to untie my boots. I knew her eyes were on me, I could feel the prickle of her awareness on my spine as I slowly rolled my jeans down my thighs, before kicking them off and striding into the water.

"Gods," I groaned, dunking my head under, slicking my hair back. A quick glance down showed Sylus and Maximus far below, sparring, wrestling, releasing some pent-up energy. The mirage of purples, blacks and blues of their scales flashed dully in the waning light. To my left Leonardo lay stretched out on his back on the bank. His tail was the only true black amongst us. And Nyx, the ethereal son of a bitch, flaunted two rings of red around his hips, the only sign of him down in the dark water.

"I'll haul them all out if you want to shift." Alek was bobbing at my side now, but I shook my head at the offer.

"They need this. Who knows when we'll get another stop to stretch out." Though my own body was protesting, I restrained the urge. As a royal, I didn't need to shift to survive. My men could only go so long, and I was going to give them all night if they wanted it.

"Cillian." Juan's voice caught my attention. He was one of the most brutal Warriors I had, but soft spoken, often remaining on the sidelines during social settings. He stood on the bank, well away from the water to not accidentally shift.

"Miss Renita will need to bathe at some point." I mentally kicked myself. Of course she would. I'm a damn moron for not even thinking of it.

"Right," I said, nodding my head. "Alek?"

"A mile ahead of you." He winked, ducking back under the water to retrieve the others. We could have our fun all night. She needed privacy. She needed to rest. She needed me to stop fucking peacocking in front of her.

"It's fine Juan." She, as if summoned by my train wreck of a thought process, had materialized at Juan's side wearing only a black bra and a pitiful excuse for underwear. I knew the groan in my throat was audible based on the way her eyes flickered to me, and the smirk that flit across her plump lips before vanishing.

"You and Mateo have done more than enough. Don't punish yourselves for my benefit. And, frankly," she snorted, rolling her eyes. "If anyone here was going to do something inappropriate, I would have been jumped in my sleep by now." Both Juan and I flinched at the notion, but the former relented, releasing a sharp whistle to his twin before they joined us in the water.

"I need to understand how you have my men wrapped around your finger like that," I said softly, keeping my gaze on the twins as they disappeared under the darkening surface. I didn't need to tread water where I was, but I still held my arms out for balance as my breath caught hearing her wade in behind me.

"Just because some people listen the first time, doesn't mean I'm some type of manipulative vixen." I couldn't help but release a snort of my own at her retort, as I'd thought as much on more than one occasion.

She swam around to face me, eyes narrowed, lips pursed. I raised a brow, just waiting patiently for her to figure out what she wanted to ask first.

"You and Aleki are clearly together." Her tone was apprehensive, but not judgmental. "So why do the pair of you keep making passes at me? Is it some kind of weird foreplay?" I released a surprised laugh, shaking my head.

"No, no. Nothing like that I assure you." I released a heavy sigh. "Yes, we are both severely attracted to you, and we've had that conversation. We've had to, on occasion, regardless of your presence." Unconsciously, my hand reaches for hers under the water, and I think we're both surprised when our fingers entwine. I lower my voice, allowing some vulnerability to seep into my tone.

"I need you to know that we do not look at you as a conquest or a means to an end. Pursuing you has been an… interesting battle of wills, but we aren't doing it because you're just an available female. If that were the case, each of us would have been entrapped in loveless marriages long ago."

My toes were still on the lakebed, so I reached out and pulled her to me, keeping her steady so she would have nothing but my words to focus on.

"I see you as the most captivating creature I've ever laid eyes on. Maybe it's the scent of witchcraft still clinging to you, mixing with your natural magic, making me high. But I look at you and suddenly every desire I've ever had becomes watered down and dull." I paused, huffing a breath. "If that is how transfixed you have made me over the course of mere days, I don't know how I'll be able to endure this once you finally allow me to get to know you."

She was shivering. I could feel it in her grip. I spared her of more teasing comments though; I was far too satisfied by the warring waves of shock, curiosity, and outrage on her face. I released my hold on her waist, let her put whatever amount of distance she felt like she needed to between us, and nodded my head in Alek's direction where he just surfaced.

"I'm sure he'll be thrilled to know you're in the loop now, but don't forget," I swam past her, just close enough to drift my fingers against her thigh if I wanted to. "Though I don't mind sharing your attention, I intend to make you mine in the end, tesoro."

I submerged while she hurled a curse at my back and laughed outright as she smacked the top of the water above me. So shy with Alek, so fiery with me. I was grateful he'd rounded up the rest of the men and brought them to shore even though initially I hadn't minded. After that exchange, shifting was the only appropriate release I would allow myself.

12

Renita

Again, I couldn't sleep. If Cora were here, I don't know who would be in more trouble: me, Cillian, or Aleki. Most likely, she would submerge me in some underwater timeout, removing me from view by force. Always keeping my secrets hidden above all else. But if she had to deal with one of the two Mer, I think Aleki would stand a better chance against her.

Unlike his counterpart, he had a suaveness; an ability to smooth over the most destructive of situations despite his given nature. I think that's why I feel relaxed in his presence. It was tangible, the sense of security which wafted off him. I could see why a man like Cillian would be attracted to a partner like that, because he was a whole other fucking problem.

It was like he baited chaos, despite being in the most danger. Calling him an adrenaline junkie didn't cover it. He was marching on one of the most haunted trails in the world while wearing Gucci for Goddess sake. His recklessness kept my hackles up, but knowing what he is was my real problem.

A royal Mer, with a tail terrifyingly similar to mine. Honest, sweet, mischievous, and irritatingly competent when he wanted to be. I knew I was not only attracted to his games, but that power held within him which he stupidly gave me a taste of. That was something Aleki would forever be protected from: my urges to take, and to feast. He would be safe if we were to—

I openly smacked my palms against my cheeks, not allowing the thought to finish its course. Poor Juan started beside me, confusion flickering in his gaze in the half-light, an orange slice halfway to his mouth.

"Sorry," I said, smoothing my hair and releasing a sigh. It was barely morning, still at least an hour before the forest would awaken the others. They had stayed up most of the night, their excitement and relief to shift keeping them whooping and wild until the witching hours. The only sounds now were the fading songs of crickets, and gentle taps of rodents across the forest floor.

"Miss Renita." Juan's voice beside me was soft, but there was an underlying sense of urgency in his tone.

"I'm okay," I started, but he held up a hand to silence me.

"I highly encourage you to get back in the water before we leave." I glanced at him sidelong, but he remained nonchalant, sucking the orange between his teeth.

"Do I smell or something?" A grin flickered across his face, and he shook his head.

"I simply wish to point out you are as pent up as the rest of us. And once we reach the curve of the Susquehanna we aim for, your opportunities for privacy will grow fewer, if not disappear completely."

Something about the phrasing made me pause, my breath catching in my chest. Juan just calmly peeled another orange, the only sound in the early morning air around us.

"What do you know?" I finally whispered, and he finally met my eyes, understanding flickering there.

"I know only two things." I bristled, power rushing down my spine in warning as he abandoned his breakfast and faced me.

"When I met you, you never looked at the water as desperately as you do now, revealing some semblance of comfort or contentment." He paused, contemplating his words. "The other fact to my eyes, is I have only met one type of Mer who can control their ability to shift." His eyes locked on me then, and the absolute devotion in his gaze almost made me crumble.

He didn't say it, but I understood his implication completely. Cillian could control his shifting. A royal Mer can control their shifting. The panic that's been slowly building in me finally crested, my heart on the verge of bursting.

A bird taking off from the branches above us had me startle, and I shot to my feet, breaths coming in gasps as my emotions overtook me. Juan catches my shoulders, not allowing me to bolt.

"Breathe Renita." The words are the harshest he's spoken to me, but they take root. He doesn't release me from his grip, breathing deeply with me until my head stops spinning.

"I am aware enough to not overstep my bounds," he said, his grip loosening. "But please… let me rest easy knowing you are well. That is all I ask of you."

The forest had begun to stir around us now, the ink-stained sky beginning to pale on the horizon. The lake glimmered when my eyes settled on it. Through the fog clinging to its surface, I could make out a water snake slithering at its edge, searching for a meal. Birds pruned their feathers in shallow puddles. Fish were kissing the surface, sucking bugs beneath.

I shuddered, scales springing to the surface of my arms, glittering like snowfall in the morning glaze. Juan said nothing, just gently guided me to the water's edge, took my shoes and shirt, and turned his back as my shaking fingers fought to rid myself of the rest of my clothes.

It took half a second to get in the water, submerging, disappearing down into the dark. A shrill sound of relief escaped me, echoing off the stones peppering the muddy bottom. This lake was not as deep as the one at home, but it was deep enough to prevent my tail from putting on any unnecessary displays as I shot through the water, twisting, soaring.

I was tempted to let it fill my lungs, to drown out the half breaths I felt myself take on land and finally *breathe*. But I paused where I was, tail drifting slowly, and instead held it in. The twin rows of angular dorsal fins that lined my spine down to the tip of my tail kept me steady as I just lingered where I was, a silver star wrapped in the waters dark embrace.

A flash of green to my left caught my attention, stomach rolling as my eyes locked on a small school of trout. I've only ever given into this a few times, and all were several years ago. But after this past week, after the amount of stress and seduction I've been entrapped in, I allowed myself the grace to break.

With a snap of my tail I was across the lake, clawed fingers grasping the fish before it realized there was a predator in the water. I knew my teeth had sharpened to points as I bit into it, feeling my fangs sinking deep as the animal thrashed. I tore a hunk of flesh from it, moaning at the fresh taste of fat and blood. I ate it clean down to the bones, the water washing away any evidence as I slowly made my way to surface.

I rolled onto my back, and let my eyes flutter shut against the rising sun. Goddess, why must this be my life? Why did you curse me so? With this power, with this newfound position of fate?

Echoing voices ricocheted off the water, causing me to still. I moved silently, submerging myself up to my eyes, scanning the shore for Juan. He was still poised, but the argument in his tone was sharp. Scared. And deep in my chest that fear echoed as my eyes placed Aleki, a few feet away, and staring straight at me.

I couldn't meet Aleki's eyes as I strode, naked, from the water. Any other day I would have been mortified, but I was far too concerned with what he may or may not have seen. Juan had a frantic look in his eyes when he followed Aleki's gaze to find me in the water, relaxing instantly as he realized I had already shifted back.

Water dripped down my legs as I waded up the bank to join them, having nowhere else to go since Juan had my clothes. Though I kept my gaze downcast, Aleki's attention washed over my skin like fire.

Was it anger, or shock maybe? If he saw my tail, there was no way to lie my way out of this. No offer I could make for him to keep it a secret from Cillian. Juan at the very least seemed intent on keeping my secret, but even that I couldn't bet on. He would be loyal to the future King before a random woman he met on the river.

"Aleki I—" before I could even finish the sentence he had eliminated the space between us, throwing a towel around my shoulders.

"I'm sorry." His words were rushed, frustration making him fumble. "I didn't intend to pry. I just woke up and realized you were gone and then Juan was being so fucking vague—"

"Aleki." His name on my lips had him snapping his jaw shut, and I found the courage to meet his gaze. "I need to know what you're doing... when you seek me out like this." His pupils dilated significantly, and I held back my sigh of relief. He didn't see. If he had, he wouldn't have been so easily distracted.

"I thought my intentions were clear," he said, releasing a chuckle. His gaze flits down again, heating slightly where the towel was bunched in my fists to hold it closed. His tone lowered, sparing Juan of the liquid honey as he whispered in my ear.

"If you wish for me to speak plainly: I'm trying to woo you, little predator."

Goosebumps tickled to life on my skin as he pressed a gentle kiss to my temple before pulling back.

"Why?" He tilted his head, as if my question made little sense.

"Well, I'll be honest. At first, I may have stoked the flames of competition with Cillian, just to see him get all worked up and going. It's been a long time since I've had to share his attention." His gaze roved over me slowly, making me feel more laid bare than I already was. "That said, I'm not blind to the appeal of his newfound taste."

"You're both nobility in need of an heir," I counter, finally finding some venom and lacing my words with it. "From my point of view, you have little other reason to pursue me." He just grinned wider.

"Well, if I were blessed to have a kit or two, I certainly wouldn't complain. But no, that's not the point. I'm unsure if you're aware, but in our world, power is not handed down through familial lines. So, on this specific note I will speak on behalf of Cillian and reassure you that neither of us has any pre-existing conditions for you. We are simply... transfixed."

He glances at Juan, some upspoken message passing between them. Juan tensed, his eyes cutting to me apologetically.

"Don't. You. Dare." I growled, watching in shock as he set my clothes down gently.

"Do you wish for me to drag him away?" Juan's question put me on the spot, and I felt my cheeks flushing. At my silence, Aleki released a sound of satisfaction.

"Fine, fine. Gods." I mumbled the words, pinching the bridge of my nose with my fingers, trying to wane off the rising blush. Juan nodded once, before quickly removing himself from the situation, heading back to the tents.

Silence stretched between Aleki and I. Slowly, I reached for my clothes, shimmying my underwear and jeans on beneath the towel. Keeping my back to him, I dropped it fully to pull on my bra. Only after my T-shirt was on did his hands find my hips, spinning me to face him. His arm hooked around my waist to press me firmly to his chest, so I had to crane my neck to look up at him.

"Why did you let Juan leave you here with me, naked and alone?" His words were hot against my face, and I groaned, pressing my hands between us into his chest.

"You expected me to make him watch this?" My words came out all rushed and he laughed.

"Fair point." His lips ghosted against my ear. "But you also could have sent me away."

My skin burned where his lips touched, slowly, gently, enough so that I knew if I struggled, he would stop immediately. I sucked in a breath as he nipped my skin, his sharpened teeth making my nerve endings dance.

"Careful little predator, the others are waking." I could feel his smile against my pulse.

"Unless you want to attract Cillian's attention? Now wouldn't that be fun if he found us?"

The idea sent a lick of heat down my spine, and Aleki tightened his grip. In a few steps he had maneuvered me backwards against the nearest tree, his lips roaming from my neck to my shoulder. Yanking the sleeve of my shirt down, he sank his teeth into me again, and this time I gasped outright. My back arched, knocking my hips into his as my hands flew to his hair, yanking on the long strands at the nape of his neck and he groaned.

His palms spread flat against my ribs, fingers digging in hard enough to steal my breath as he steadied me against him. It had been a while, but I could tell even through our clothes, his erection was impressively sized.

"I will stop." His voice was hoarse as his fingers played with the edges of my shirt, exposing the skin on my hip. "But I'd very much prefer if you allowed me to relieve some of the tension in your body."

Before I could even form a question, he was moving south, slowly trailing a line of kisses down my chest as he knelt at my feet. My eyes widened as he undid my zipper, sliding my jeans down, pressed an open mouth kiss over my panties.

"D-do you even know what you're—"

"If you think we live underwater with tails out all the time then you're insane." He cut me off, yanking my panties down next. His breath was hot against my exposed clit, and instantly my legs tensed. The grin on his lips was wicked. "Spread your legs."

He pressed a hand against my inner thigh, urging me wider, and then his tongue was on me. I tried to hold in my moan, the sound leaving me strained and desperate. One of my hands left his hair to cover my mouth as a finger joined his tongue, sinking into me at the same moment he sucked my clit between his teeth.

I rolled my hips, past the point of reservation. Between the two of them, I'd been worked up and on edge more in the past week than I had been in my entire life. His grunt of approval vibrated my core, making it clench tighter around his finger as it curled to stroke my most sensitive place.

"That's it." The encouragement was a growl against my skin.

I cried out beneath my hand, stars sparking at the edge of my vision as he began to work me faster. I was full on grinding against his tongue now, the pleasure white hot when he added a second finger, stretching me further. My legs buckled, but he just kept thrusting his fingers faster, replacing his mouth with his thumb to work my clit in tight, fast circles.

"Such a sweet girl when you're honest, little predator. Go ahead," he growled, kissing my inner thigh. "Cum for me Renita. I need to see you break from just my touch."

I damn near screamed, the combination of his touch and his words hurtling me over the edge. I gasped for breath, melting back against the tree as I felt my walls pulsing around his fingers, continuing to stroke me long and slow until the last ripples of my orgasm faded.

I heard a twig snap and whipped my head up, instantly finding Cillian's gaze. His jaw was slack, darkened eyes glued to Aleki who placed one final kiss on my abused clit, making me jump again. We both tracked his every move as he picked up the fallen towel, taking his time to clean between my legs before shifting my panties back in place. When he stood, he pulled my jeans with them, the zipper and button sounding like canon fire over the morning birdsong.

"Do you wish to know how she tastes, my King?" He asked, voice low. My pussy clenched again as I cut my gaze back to Cillian, who's pale skin had taken on a rosy hue.

"Yes," he said breathlessly. Aleki smirked wider, turning from me to Cillian. His hand laced around the back of his head, pulling him closer and he closed his mouth over his. As his tongue parted Cillian's lips my legs finally gave out, and I sank to the ground, watching as Cillian moaned and sucked my juices off Aleki's tongue.

"Good boy," Aleki growled, pressing his fingers to his mouth next. Cillian shivered, wrapping his arms around Aleki's waist, eyes shut while he sucked his fingers clean.

"You see how much he also craves you, little predator?" I knew I had to be gaping at them, just as well as I knew a fresh wave of wetness dampened my panties.

"W-we need to keep going," I said, still out of breath and disoriented. Aleki shrugged, pulling his fingers free from Cillian's mouth, slapping his cheek gently.

"You heard the woman. Time to get a move on and hopefully get off these blasted mountains."

Cillian looked like he was spiraling as much as I was, protest written all over his features, but there was a sense of complacency as well.

"Right." He coughed, untangling himself from Aleki, holding the back of his hand to his mouth. "The others were waking when I left. We can get moving quickly."

Both their eyes were on me, and I realized I was still sunk onto the ground, wet and stunned. On shaking legs I stood, darting past them to retrieve my boots and coat. I pulled it on, zipping it up as if the extra layer could do anything to erase what just happened.

13

Renita

I didn't look at anybody after returning to camp. Instead, I marched to my tent, grabbed the one oblong bag that I hadn't opened yet, and marched straight past the breakfast campfire. I had to admit, I was a little proud of them for finally figuring out how to light it on their own, but I didn't stop to comment on it.

The bag I carried was the only one I refused to allow them to take, its contents delicate and light. But deadly, which I was counting on.

I'd detached it from my tent bag yesterday after the gallantry that was everyone taking my stuff, and had held it close like my life depended on it. The Mer had been very confused but hadn't asked questions. Unlike now.

The number of squawking protests as I marched down the mountain trail alone was actually quite humorous. I didn't get far before I heard heavy footfalls racing after me, and I braced myself for Aleki or Cillian to whip me around. Shockingly, it was Nyx who threw himself in front of me, arms spread and eyes wide with concern.

"Where are you going?" He asked. Leonardo materialized at his side, looking more disgruntled with me than worried.

"We need more food, and I don't suppose any of you know how to hunt on land?" I asked. Silently, Nyx dropped his arms, and Leonardo was suddenly fascinated by the foliage. I sighed, unzipping the bag. "Yea, that's what I thought."

I lifted the bow, a sleek, black thing I've had for years, out of the bag. Growing up on the run, my mother taught me many ways to survive, even if they were gross. What berries and plants I could eat, which animals to trap or track, and how to field dress them when necessary. The bow was one of the only things I had left that was from her, a gift for my seventh birthday. It should have been too big, the weight too heavy for a child to pull. But as I was a Siren, it had been perfect.

"We won't reach a safe place to descend the mountains for another two days. Three if your precious nobles lallygag," I grumbled, lifting the quiver of arrows and hanging it off my shoulder. I shoved the empty bag into Leonardo's arms despite the frown he wore.

"Our credit cards will come in handy once we reach the coast, but we need to survive the mountain first. So, with luck, I'm going to find a buck, lure him in, and we'll have plenty of meat for the rest of the trip. So long as Leo here is strong enough to carry it."

"Watch it," he warned, voice tense, but Nyx wore the faintest smile.

"Right. I guess that makes sense. Do you want us to—"

"No," I said, shaking my head. "I won't go far, just enough to where its quiet. A group as large as ours would spook anything away for several miles."

Nyx looked torn, but Leonardo was more than happy to oblige the request. He dropped a large palm on the Warriors shoulder, urging him to the side so I could pass.

"I won't be longer than an hour," I promised him, before turning on my heel and disappearing into the trees.

For the first time in weeks, I could take a full breath. The forest was my home, despite my blood. I knew a part of me would shatter once we finally reached the sea. I feared another part of me, the one that was depraved, would be far too enchanted to care about my breaking heart.

In short time I found a deer trail, dropping my boots at the head, and tiptoeing barefoot across the dirt. I followed its tangled path through the brush, letting my senses flow out, pupils dilating, ears perking. The forest spoke a language very few could understand. It was old, a cacophony of riddles and whispers which overflowed themselves to the point of disorientation. Humans, if they tried to listen, would often become drunk on it, and lost to their world. Fae could interpret, for a price. I however, could manipulate its chorus to my favor.

It started out as a hum, the song in my chest, one powerful enough to silence the bird's overhead. The only sound besides my own was the rising wind, the world answering my call. My eyes drifted shut as my lips parted, the sound old, and dripping with temptation. I felt the earth shivering beneath me, the life in the roots of the trees extending towards my touch, my dark promise. It was an effort not to forget myself, to notch an arrow to the bow, and wait.

I could feel the hoof steps beneath my feet, the adamant snorting of the buck, long before he appeared at the edge of the trees. He was young, strong, the evidence ringing his neck and shoulders in faint scars from the antlers of others who invaded his territory. His strength would not help him here.

My song crested as I leased the arrow, the shrill call of my voice racing in tandem besides the singing of the bowstring. The arrow pierced its throat, my breath catching as I watched the blood spurt, the life end.

I didn't approach the body right away, needing to collect myself. Just the sight of the blood urged me towards a frenzy, my canines sharpening, my nails elongating to claws. I didn't have this reaction as a child, this manifested as my powers grew, and my stomach lurched with fear as I realized I still needed to gut the thing before carrying it back to camp.

Sweeping the bow over my shoulders, I forced myself to descend the short hill too where it lay. Kneeling by its side, my instincts screamed to let my claws slice its belly open, but my shaking fingers retrieved the knife from my pocket, making the long even cut with a blade instead.

The stink of half-digested stomach rot snapped me out of my stupor, and I made quick work of the rest. My hands and jeans were bloodstained by the time I was done, but it was prepared for the trek back to the others. I paused, clenching its hooves in my fists, suddenly torn.

I could just disappear right now. These mountains were known for absorbing you alive, human or not. So long as they followed the trail, the Mer would find their way to the river, and from there back to the sea. They could fight their own war.

"You're not seriously considering carrying that thing yourself?" I whipped around, the sharp voice at my back full of judgement. Leonardo was braced against a tree across the clearing from me, eyeing the corpse at my feet with a frown. "I'll begrudgingly admit you're strong, but that thing weighs at least twice as you do."

"What are you doing here?" His gaze snapped to mine, burning in annoyance at my accusing tone.

"You openly mocked me in front of my Warrior," he growled, pushing off the tree and prowling to my side. "Or did you forget?"

"I wasn't—" I sighed, deciding not to argue. Though I hadn't meant it offensively, of course he took it personally. These damn Mer, so fixated on protocol and decorum that they couldn't glean sarcasm. And, if he arrived any sooner, I would have been caught. Leonardo, oblivious to my concerns, just side-stepped me, kneeling beside the carcass and hoisting it over his shoulder in a single fluid motion.

"I followed you to help." Though still gruff, his tone had gentled microscopically, like he felt guilty for sneaking around despite my clear request to do this on my own. "You'd said you wanted me to carry it. So, I waited, then followed your scent before it faded so I could fulfill the request."

A bolt of surprise and then shame washed through me. I'd glamoured him. That was the only explanation for why he would have followed, after so visibly detesting my presence. He stood as if the weight of the animal was nothing, eyes finding mine again.

"I don't understand why I am driven to help you. It's a nuisance." His admission made my nerves run cold, and I averted my gaze.

"Well, truthfully neither do I." It was the best parry I could come up with, and I didn't wait for a reply. We made our way back up the trail in silence, only pausing so that I could tug on my boots. By the time we reached camp, the sun was high, and the men were bored. Lucky me.

14

Cillian

I broke after she'd gone, finally reaching my limit, and Alek was far too pleased to indulge me. My men made themselves scarce, a few trailing Renita I think, just to make sure she was safe, but I could no longer focus on that tempest of a woman with Alek's cock down my throat.

In the early stages of our relationship, it was embarrassing. Alek himself had seemed genuinely surprised that I, the future King, was more than willing to be submissive. It was more than being willing though: I needed it. I absolutely fucking craved letting go of the control I was expected to wield and have the pressures on my shoulders literally pounded out of me.

I saw stars as he thrust in deeper, the head of his cock choking me and I groaned at the sensation, my eyes fluttering shut. I still had her damn taste on my tongue, a wicked honey which was mixing with Alek's saltiness into a dangerously addictive cocktail. I began palming myself through my jeans, desperate for any type of relief, and heard Alek's low chuckle above me.

"Need to cum just from this, my King?" He paused his movements, deliberately letting his velvet soft head linger on my tongue as it leaked precum. I shuddered and he gripped my chin hard, easing himself free.

I couldn't help but pant as he joined me on the mossy forest floor. His fingers moved deftly; each touch was precise as he rid me of my clothes. His mouth roamed from my pulse to my torso, those damn teeth of his dragging hard enough to leave red lines against my pale skin, before sinking into my hipbone and making me jerk.

"Awe, I know your excited." His voice was a purr against my skin as he forced me down, spreading my legs to settle between them. The head of his cock was still dripping with my saliva as he nudged it against my opening, easing himself inside in one smooth thrust. His mouth found mine again as he began to move, his free hand urging one of mine to grip my length. I growled against his lips, not wanting to cum yet, but his answering groan told me he wasn't going to give me a choice.

"Alek... wait..." I panted, my free hand dragging down his spine.

"Whatever for?" He tightened his grip on my fist, forcing me to jerk myself harder, faster. Our bodies slapping together was the only sound besides the birdsong. My breaths turned ragged as he rolled his thumb across my tip, painting it with my precum. A satisfied groan rumbled from his

chest to mine, and he started thrusting into me
harder.

"You're already dripping Cillian. Soak me
fully, let me know I've satisfied you."

Pleasure shot through me, my legs
clenching around his hips as I bucked into his
hand, coming apart. Threads of my cum painted
us, a shattered moan breaking from me as Alek
sank to the hilt, his length pulsing with his own
release.

We lay there for a few moments in silence,
wrapped around each other in the dappled
sunlight. Alek's heart was racing, mine echoing
the rush.

"You're an asshole," I groaned, shifting my
hips, and he chuckled as he slid free.

"I simply wished to give you relief. Sorry
for not playing with you longer." He was smirking
as I shoved him off me, reaching for my jeans to
yank them back on.

"Not that." I ran a hand through my hair,
shaking the twigs free, blushing as I realized my
pale locks were most defiantly stained with the
earth. "You set this up." His smile was wicked,
and unapologetic. I frowned deeper but allowed
him to tilt my head, capturing my mouth again.

"Is that a complaint?" He asked, hands
skimming my shirt, rebuttoning it for me. "Should
I not have woken you with my touch? Should I not
have encouraged you to find me?" He lowered his

voice, pressing his lips to my ear. "Did you dislike seeing my tongue in her cunt?"

My length throbbed once in response, and I clenched my jaw, forcing a swallow. He placed one last kiss on my mouth before stepping back, relieving me of some of the heat threatening to drown me.

"I fully intend to push you both, until one of you tells me to stop." A shiver wracked through me, but I said nothing. He pulled on his jeans then, glancing at me over his shoulder with a half grin. "And considering I got to taste both of your cum before breakfast, I think you know how this is going to continue to progress. Regardless of if you're mentally prepared for it."

My mind was a mess, and I couldn't find an argument. I twisted, stalking through the trees, ignoring his warm laughter as he followed. We'd been gone far longer than I realized, because as I stomped my way back to my tent the scent of cooking meat hit my nose. And then blood.

At first, my stomach curdled, seeing Renita's bloodstained hands. I was by her side before I even realized it, yanking her by the shoulder to spin her around, eyes roving over every inch of her. Her expression morphed from shock to annoyance, mouth moving but I heard nothing as I searched her for whatever wound stained half her body with blood.

"Renita—"

"She is well." I finally acknowledge Leonardo by her side, and the half-skinned buck dangling from the tree behind him. Slowly, my heartrate descended to its normal cadence, the ringing in my ears subsiding.

"I apologize," I half whisper, releasing my death grip on her at once. Her eyes became wells of hesitation, and something else, something softer. Like she was pleased by my obsession with her care, because it truly was an obsession now. I had just moved like a man possessed.

"Well damn." Alek sidled up beside me, eyeing the buck with clear satisfaction. "It seems our little predator was successful on her hunt."

"Of course I was!" She snapped, tossing her hair as she turned away from us, her strokes with the knife as sure and precise as Alek's touch on my body. "Someone needs to keep you damn fools alive."

There was something buried deep in her muttered words, an undertow dragging me in. She cared. And she fucking hated it. I knew I was grinning because of the look Leonardo gave me, but I couldn't care less.

"Very considerate, tesoro." She bristled against the endearment, and I chuckled. I shifted my gaze from her to the small fire on the other side of the tree. My men were squatted around it, the lot of them cackling and poking at each other like they were once again kits.

"What are... you having them do?" I
branched the question out, trying to mask my
concern with how close they were to open flame.

"They're cooking." She said it simply, as if
everything that was ever consumed had to be
charred by flame first. I felt her eyes on me, that
cool gaze piercing me, but softening. "Most meat
from mammals on land will make you sick. Not
everything can be served as sushi."

"Right." I didn't bother trying to explain
our eating habits, she would learn on her own in
due time. Right now, I was focused on keeping my
breathing even as she abandoned her knife, slowly
curling towards my side like an eel circling the
pointed edge of a reef. Curiosity and wariness at
war.

"I tasked them all to go find a stick just
slightly thinner than their pinkie fingers." Her
voice when it was void of rage and judgement was
like the sweetest music. "That got them to work
off some pent up energy." I should be whipped for
my thoughts on pent up energy. "And after dicing
the meat, I have them smoking it over the fire.
They decided to make a competition out of it all
their own, whose meat will cook the fastest." She
paused, then added in a tone so gentle I could
have kissed her, "I've reminded them to be careful
many times."

"Goddess, you torcher me." Her eyes found
mine, wide and... "You truly enjoy seeing me
miserable," I added, narrowing my gaze on the

clearly pleased smirk curving her lips. The vixen just shrugged.

"I don't understand your obsession with me." Her blunt words caught me off guard, my next breath stuck in my throat.

"I've been trying to work it out. At first, I thought it was just a natural pull since you're the future King. Then I thought it was just pent-up male energy, but now knowing your relationship with Aleki," her cheeks noticeable ripened at the mention of his name, which made me simultaneously jealous and complicit. Before I could even muster the amount of confidence to clear my throat she turned towards me, jabbing her finger into my chest once more.

"I can even understand the willingness to share my body," she hissed, and by now I was certain my face was redder than hers. "But I can *feel* the difference between you two, Cillian. I know Aleki's advances are genuine, but the way he approaches, damn near commanding my attention whereas you..." she trails off, faltering for the first time on her rant.

"I what?" My whisper seems to shock her, making her flinch, making goosebumps appear on her toned skin. I lean closer, taking in her scent again, and I can't believe how much I love the smell of the earth and muddy water when it's on her. "What am I doing to you, Renita?"

"Haunting me." The breathless way she said it, I knew there was desire there. But for some reason, fear was outweighing it.

I grabbed her hand, careful of the fingers which had shifted to claws, and for the thousandth time wondered if there was any way I could return her tail to her. It was clear she was strong, and powerful. She'd not only survived a curse meant to kill her, but had honed her remaining magic into something so sharp it rivaled my own at times. And yet, there she stood, trembling like a stalk of seaweed moments before it's torn from its perch by a rogue wave.

"If you could forget my position for half of a moment, do you think you could feel more than fear or disdain in my presence?" I asked quietly, my voice hushed to the same tone I use with my nieces when their brothers made them cry.

"Yes." Her answer was instant, as were her next words. "And I fucking hate it."

"Mhm." My mouth finds her temple and she doesn't move, accepting the gentle kiss I lay there. "You don't hate me."

She didn't argue, and I didn't push. Instead, I led her away from the carcass hanging behind her, dampened a towel, and wiped her arms free of blood. Then I disappeared into the refuge of my tent without another word.

15

Renita

Cillian did not leave his tent for the remainder of the day— which only lengthened this damn trek.

What was I doing? I no longer knew. At first, it was out of desperation that I joined the Mer. There was some curiosity, who could blame me, but I prioritized protecting my Coven above all. The Sirens would keep coming the longer he stayed there. And as much as he wanted the help of the Witches, the night of the water festival proved we would be of little to no aid.

But how far would this take me? I doubted they would just let me lead them out of the hills and drop them off on the beach. Yet, they thought I had no tail. Perhaps that could garner some sympathy and get me out of joining them... wherever the hell their kingdom was.

I very largely doubted that as well, and not only because of Aleki and Cillian. All of the Mer, whether they noticed it or not, were beginning to garner for my favor through approval or friendship. It would be difficult to convince the group as a whole to let me go and never see me again once all this was over.

And how would it end? Bloodshed, most likely. If I wasn't caught, I was almost certain I would be expected to slaughter my own kin. Now I'm not going to fib myself into believing that the Sirens weren't the vicious creatures everyone in my life claimed them to be. I watched them attack my home, nearly drowning a townful of innocents. I've felt the heady pull of my own power and nearly been swept under time and time again. And yet... I knew not nearly enough to want to kill them.

The Mer killed my mother. They wouldn't hesitate to kill me, no matter how pleased they were by my presence now. The Sirens kill everyone. Or do they hide like me? And kill before being killed?

The wail of a screech owl interrupted my midnight thoughts, derailing the rushing train of them before they could consume me whole. I started upright, out of that half-awake half-asleep state. A sheen of sweat made my skin glow in the tempered lantern light, making my curls stick to my shoulders. I don't know if I needed air or water, but this tent was suddenly too damn small.

"Renita?" I would have screamed if not for Cillian's palm over my mouth the second I threw the flap of my tent open. His wide eyes were dark storms in the night, the irises glittering with the faintest, most tantalizing sheen of lilac. "What's wrong? You were crying out in your sleep."

I yanked his hand off my mouth, but before I could fumble for an excuse or chastise him the screech owl sounded again. But it was wrong… guttural.

Mimicry.

"Oh, Gods no," I breathed out, yanking him into the tent behind me, whipping a blade from my boot. Fear laced every inch of my nerves, making my palms prickle with apprehension and barely contained power. "Please, please, no." I begged in a whisper, ignoring Cillian's hands steadying my waist as I stood. I lashed out, kicking him firmly in the chest to make him fall backwards to my sleeping bag.

"Stay in the tent."

"Renita?" Aleki's tired voice drifted from my right, his tent flap zipping open and a strangled sound of desperation left me, making both the men freeze.

"Stay. In. The. Tents." I didn't bother to mask the glamour, my Siren song free flowing into my urgent whisper. I'd heard the others begin to rouse, the telltale shifting of boots and zippers, but at the call in my voice, all fell silent. Except for the chewing.

I didn't bother to tiptoe— it knew we were here. Rounding the corner of my tent I froze, terror gripping me as I took in the sight not five feet from me.

Standing on its hind legs and tearing into what remained of the buck I'd shot earlier, was a deer. A grey dear, with its own meat hanging off it in loose flaps. Pointed teeth like a coyotes tore into the flesh and a single dead, white eye stared at me while it ate. From deep within its throat, it let loose that gurgling fake screech as it lowered to all fours, taking jerking steps in my direction.

"Don't come any closer." I'm unsure now if my song is for the men in the tents, or the creature before me, but the creature doesn't stop. Its tongue, much too long, and as white as its eyes, licks the knife I've extended. It's resounding hiss churns the ice in my veins to molten lava.

This wasn't the first skin walker I've encountered. But this was the first one I would have to kill. Monsters like us, when we cross paths, typically just continue on. But this time we were surrounded by prey. Magical prey, which would satiate beings like us for months.

Not happening.

Its startled screech when I drove the blade into its skull made my ears ring. That wouldn't kill it. Something this old, this dark, needed to be shredded to pieces— discarded in parts so it couldn't drag its blackened soul back together again.

I stab blindly with the knife, ignoring the claws which puncture my ribcage. Black blood oozes from its wounds, staining my skin and the forest floor, running in the sudden downpour to tint everything it touches. The earth gives way beneath our feet as the blade breaks free of its hideous hide, its gangly grey limbs tumbling end over end down the ravine with me close behind.

I let out a shout as I landed on a log, feeling the skin on my hip break open. The walker was up again, the bones of its shoulder protruding from its flesh but it seemed to not notice as it dove atop me. We wrestled in the mud, all flashing claws and teeth. I could barely see anything anymore, the darkness of the woods and the added blurred vision from the storm that came out of nowhere was more than enough to overload my senses.

I screamed outright when it tore a hunk of flesh from my leg with its teeth. Something inside me snapped at that. My nails lengthened to true claws, curved and black as my arms rounded the creature's torso to dig into its spine. I felt its vertebra shredding beneath my touch, clinging to its bucking body as I fisted the root of its spine and tore it away from its hips.

A bolt of lightning hits the log, throwing us apart. But I crawled back, the raw power of the storm fueling my rage, and my hunger. The walker was heavier than me but could barely fight as I pinned it down. I laughed against its scream as I tore its exposed spine from its body, and the fight left it. Next were the arms, the feet, one leg, both. And then my teeth were in its neck, biting, shredding, sucking, until it dangled at an obscure angle. I sliced it off with the blade, then rolled off the carcass, my body steaming as it tried and failed to heal itself.

I didn't need to look down to know that whatever was left of my tail had appeared. I'd lost too much blood, called too much power, and was lying in a muddy water filled ditch. Lightening flickered again, and another laugh tore from my hoarse throat. Was this how I'd die, following in similar fashion to my mother? At least when she fell from the cliff, she was met by the deep embrace of the sea, whereas I was about to be buried in the earth. A hell, I realized, no matter how much I meant it when I called it my home.

"My Gods..." I couldn't place the voice, or the face for that matter. My vision was blurred by the rain, the black, the faint pulse of violet before I sank into nothing.

16

Renita

I didn't want to wake up, that first wave of pain yanking me towards the verge of puking before I'd even cracked my eyes.

"Easy there, alteza." Warm hands found my shoulders, gentle against the blossoming bruises. "Please don't jerk, we finally got the bleeding to stop."

I peeled my eyes open, squinting up at Juan, whose warm smile clashed harshly with the agony in my body.

"What—"

"You passed out in the ravine, after killing the creature." His hands smoothed down my arms, which I just realized were bandaged from the wrists to almost my shoulders. "You must relax so your body can heal."

The hush of water had me trying to sit up, but as gentle as his touch was, it remained firm. I could feel my scales kissing the skin of my lower belly, finally realizing I was in a pool of some kind. Panic flooded me, and my tail whipped, splashing roughly against the curve of the tub and drawing a curse from Mateo who hovered a few feet away.

His hands dove beneath the warm water, a flurry of apologies before I was crying out at his touch. It felt like I was on fire, whatever peel or gauze he was reapplying making the bite out of my side scream in agony.

"Alteza please," Juan begged. "You don't need to panic. You mustn't—"

"D-don't look," it was my turn to beg, tears falling freely as my scales reflected off the pale walls in a shimmering array of prismatic light.

"Renita." Mateo dried his hands, coming to my other side and I cried harder. Whether they looked or not they knew. They knew I'd been lying. They knew the damning color of my scales. They knew—

"My Queen, there is no need to cry." I could barely even process his words; all the pent-up emotions were overflowing at once. The water sloshed again, and aggravated, I forced them to let me sit up this time, to take in where we were.

We were definitely in a house, most likely still near the trail. It wasn't uncommon in these parts for families to rent out their houses or bedrooms to hikers, but I doubt they would want their jacuzzi used for this purpose.

The thing was large enough to accommodate not only my whole tail, but the mountain of wet towels at my back, which is how I was propped up on a soft surface. Despite my trembling the water was warm, tinted just slightly pink from the wound on my side which was wrapped tightly with…

"Seaweed? Are you kidding me?" I don't know why that's what drew the rage out of me, but it was. The mirror cracked from the energy spike in the room, the sounds of tinkling glass filling the space. Mateos hand was firmly on my shoulder now, easing me back.

"Not exactly. Built of it yes, but it's a medicinal wrap. We had several packed."

"Shut up!" I snapped, running my hands through my wet hair. Juan had fallen quiet, his gaze flicking from my tail to the door and back again. His eyes found his brothers, burning. Mateo gave the slightest shake of his head, and my answering growl was enough to make them both flinch.

"Cillian." My voice flowed around the room, my anger curbing my songs urge to manifest.

There was a soft click as the door behind me opened, and in the shattered remnants of the mirror I watched him step into the room. Juan and Mateo had shifted subtly, putting a distance between us that wasn't there since I woke.

"You may go." His voice was gentle, warm, but the command in it was unmissable. We just stared at each other in the broken mirror as the brothers puttered for a moment longer, mumbled something about my bandages, and left, shutting the door softly behind them.

I'd been naked in front of Cillian before, but somehow, this experience was worse. He crossed the room to me slowly and leaned against the edge of the tub, careful not to touch me. I kept my gaze glued to the shattered glass, unable to meet his eyes as he sat there, studying me.

"You've risked your life for us twice now," he murmured, fingers finally reaching out to tuck one of my curls behind my ear. "Why are you so willing to die, but so unwilling to—"

"Do not finish that question." My words were whispered but cracked like a whip, and after a moments pause, he smiled.

"Mi tesoro," he cupped my cheek, lifting me gently but I still refused to look at him. I was waiting for the blow, the anger, the accusations, but they didn't come. Instead, he sighed, rolling his thumb across my wet cheek.

"You have no idea what you are, do you?" My whole body went rigid at the question. Was it a trap? He wouldn't be laughing then, right? Wouldn't be smiling so warmly, be getting so close if he thought—

My brain short circuited as he kissed me, the touch so brief, so gentle, I thought I imagined it at first.

"Forgive me," was his instant words, so baffling I couldn't speak. "I expect nothing of you, absolutely nothing. But I needed just one. If anything, to feel less alone with the weight I carry."

"Weight?" I scrunched my brow, "What? Cillian—"

"You are a royal, Renita." When my gaze met his, his eyes were full violet. Unwavering, unyielding, unguarded by the storms. "Chosen by the Gods to rule, as I have been. This secret will stay with us, and my men. Nothing will be expected of you, unless you want it."

"But..." I didn't recognize my own voice, wet and broken. "I lied."

I'd done so much more than that, he wouldn't forgive me if he knew to what extent. What darkness I harbored. What thrill I got tearing that wendigo apart in my bare hands.

"Yes." He swallowed, shifting back. "I don't think I'll ever fully understand the extent of how you came to live on a mountain, considering what you are. At the very least your parents would have—"

"My father abandoned my mother before I was born." There it was, that sharp edge to my tone I so desperately needed right now. Lilac eyes on me, patient, listening. "I don't even know if he was a Mer, and if he was, she never revealed what role he had to play in your twisted society." At this his brows pinched, a frown curbing his mouth.

"Twisted?"

"You kill your own kind." I glared at him, every ounce of misery in my blood being thrown at him in that look. "I understand the functioning differences between Mer and Sirens. But I don't understand why one gets to murder the other, before they even realize what they are. I don't understand why those who escape the slaughter, are hunted and criminalized simply for existing with powers they didn't ask for."

Cillian, if possible, had gone paler than normal, his skin taking on an icy sheen similar to his hair. I leaned up again, ignoring the pain in my body. "My mothers lack of understanding, and the daring tongue to ask the questions I just spat at you, landed *her* cursed. My tail wasn't taken by Sirens, as we led you to believe. Hers was taken by the Mer, before they drowned her for daring to question your politics." It was the closest to the truth I could ever tell him.

"So yes. I have looked at you barely concealing my disgust. Because the crown you'll wear one day is stained with her blood, and the blood of the children labeled monsters before they could even properly swim!"

Cillian hadn't moved as my voice rose. Hadn't flinched when my hand grasped his wrist, nails digging in. The only change had been his eyes briefly shuttering, but now they practically glow with restrained power.

"Renita." I flinched, but he shushed me, prying my fingers off his wrist. "I'm afraid I may be revoking a few of my promises." My heart was thudding so hard I could see faint ripples on the water when my eyes shot down, a new sense of fear embracing me.

They didn't need to find out I was a Siren to kill me. They never actually caught my mother, suspicion was enough. She never used her magic in my entire lifetime, but the fact she had it was enough. And I just stepped onto the same plank, questioning, arguing, fighting.

"I may need to force the ring on your finger, but I won't rule with anyone else by my side." This time when he touched me, his grip was unwavering, yanking my gaze to his.

"I cannot be your Queen—"

"You are already a Queen! Me being by your side does not dictate your place!"

He never so much as raised his voice at me till now, his grip on my chin softening just enough for his thumb to trail over the pearl under my lip.

"I refuse to rule at court beside anyone else. Be it a husband, ally, friend, or enemy. I am the one the Sirens are attempting to kill." His words made me wince now, guilt creeping in behind the fear. "But I would be a fool to assume that an entire race of people wants me dead, simply because they are evil.”

The storm inside my head instantly died, and the crackling energy in the room silenced. There was nothing but my rushing blood, and our heavy breaths.

“Though everyone in the Oceans may be trying to convince me of that painful simplicity, it cannot be true.” His voice cracked slightly, and this time when he pulled away, he stood, pacing out his own anxiety.

“The creature that attacked us last night was evil. The Sirens, vicious as they are, are organized. They plan. They talk. There is something bigger at play, otherwise they would just hunt and kill at random.”

“You didn’t express these views the first time we discussed—”

“You just said my people killed your mother for questioning it,” he snapped, whipping his head to face me. “Imagine what they would do to me.”

The future King, a traitor to their ways. Handing himself over to the enemy. Wanting to understand them. And with me by his side, they would never believe his innocence.

“You’re right about one thing,” I murmur, licking my lips. His eyes track the movement, jaw ticking. I flick my tail slowly, a ray of light from my iridescent scales crossing his face, but he doesn't even squint. That stirs something low in my belly.

"Well, are you going to tell me, or remain all cryptic?" He asks, annoyance lacing the words. For the first time in days, I feel myself smiling, before a laugh tumbles out of me.

"You will indeed have to force that ring on my finger. I will not take a throne willingly."

17

Renita

I'd been right about our whereabouts. The cottage we were in sat at the base of the mountain, a few hundred yards from the trail. I had drastically miscalculated how far we'd already travelled though. These past weeks, it felt like we'd walked at a snail's pace, the Mer needing frequent breaks and being fascinated by every twig sticking out of the ground causing several childlike delays. I was pleasantly surprised when Nyx alerted me the next morning that we'd reach our self-imposed rendezvous on the Susquehanna in a day— hours if we loaded ourselves into the two G Wagons which Cillian procured... somehow.

Shockingly, Leonardo was the only one on my side when I argued against traveling by car. The whole reason we had been walking to begin with was to alleviate the damage if the Sirens found us again. A car accident on the highway could kill somebody, and I didn't want their blood on our hands because of some supernatural feud.

That argument was dismissed almost immediately, since other than Leonardo, each of them had begun behaving like I was made of glass. If Cillian's consistent hovering weren't enough, Aleki had even softened, his teases morphing to an elegant grace a man his stature shouldn't be capable of. Mateo and Juan remained relatively the same, only because they had been doting on me since they met me. But having Nyx, the once rough and solitary Mer now going out of his way to quietly advise and mitigate arguments, along with Maximus and Sylus morphing their typical brute and foxlike characteristics as well, it was all too obvious what they were doing. And I hated it. By the third morning, my patience and tolerance and attempts to understand had evaporated completely.

"In case you all forgot, I took care of it!" The kitchen fell quiet as I tore the bandages off my leg. The skin had healed over nicely the past few days, which was the only reason I hadn't been man handled back into the jacuzzi this morning. Something about the 'natural state' of my body which I had zero interest in entertaining.

The wound, though closed and not infected, was still clear as day. Where my skin usually drank in the sun's warmth, this area stood pale, new, soft to the touch. And they clucked like a group of hens over it because they couldn't dare risk the welfare of a royal.

"I am more than capable of walking in this state. If we leave now, we'll reach the river by tomorrow afternoon, hitch a ride on a passing train, and then get to hop on one of the summer float trips—"

"Or you can just get in the car, and we'll make our cruise in time." Cillian cut me off, his smile like liquid honey.

"Cruise?" I asked skeptically, unsure if I heard him right, and if I did if I even wanted to know what ridiculous thing he threw money at now.

"Yes. I rented a boat." He looked completely, overly self-satisfied.

"And before you worry that pretty little head of yours," Aleki interjected, materializing behind me with his hands on my shoulders. "Maximus and Sylus did some digging, and procured it from a... medicine man?"

"Shamen," Maximus said with a huff. "Native man. Insisted on connecting our spirits to the boat or some shit."

"Something about pure waters and blessed travels," Sylus added unhelpfully from across the breakfast bar, dipping an apple slice into a plastic carton of caramel. "In simpler terms, I believe he did something like a protection spell. Considering what we've been through already, I welcome the sentiment."

"If the Sirens have tracked me, they would have attacked while we rested here." The arrogance from Cillian's voice had morphed back to that serene calm, how I would imagine the shush of a gentle tide against wet sand. He sighed, adding gently, "Though I'm inclined to agree, the sentiment is nice. And the form of travel much more preferred than continuing to abuse my poor feet on these trails."

For the first time in my life, I simply couldn't argue. Maybe he was glamouring me, but I sat, shrugging off Aleki's touch and stared into my mug of coffee.

Leonardo finished cooking the remaining deer meat, stirred together with eggs from the fridge and thyme Sylus had picked in the garden. If I closed my eyes, I could pretend I was back at the diner, with Maria singing along poorly to the crackling radio and Alice shouting order numbers when they were ready. I sipped my coffee, feeling Nyx, my new shadow, leaning against the counter by my side.

"Let me guess," I murmured, keeping my gaze on the drink in my hand. "You also want to implore your Queen to think with reason for her safety."

"Yes." I glared at him and his mouth twitched, his version of a smile. "But I also wanted to remind her of why we are together. This trip was intended to find aid for the King, and I'd rather not risk dangling him in front of the jaws of another beast. Or be ordered to watch my Queen risk herself to kill it again."

My fingers tightened on the mug, guilt roiling through me. They thought I'd glamoured them into submission, but it was really a Siren song. Something I only managed to hide, because of my tail. Why… why was I both? How was it even possible? A monster ordained by a God to… what? Was my purpose to rule, or to destroy?

"Renita?" His eyes were on me, cold, yet concerned, and I heaved a sigh.

"Damn it, Nyx," I grumbled, my gaze sliding to the two men across the room who finally looked away from me long enough to reassure one another. "At the very least, don't put me in a car with them. If I'm really so weak and feeble they shouldn't have the opportunity to paw at me in close quarters."

Nyx laughed.

"I wouldn't have minded," I say for the third time since we departed. Not that I would have been over the moon about it, but I was the smallest. I should have been the one perched in the middle of the twins, not poor Leonardo.

I wasn't shocked when Juan and Mateo herded me towards one of the cars. But I was surprised when the rest of the Mer began arguing over who else would be coming.

Nyx had been right at my heels, but Leonardo had been trailing Cillian. Apparently, paired power partners (or whatever the hell they wanted to call themselves) were not flexible in the Mer world like they were in the Coven.

It was more of a bond here, a connection that couldn't be undone or shifted unless one of them died. Momentarily I panicked that Cillian would pull that card as I, a 'Manipulative', pulled his magic from him as a Siphon just a few weeks ago. My sigh of relief was audible when he climbed in the backseat of the other G Wagon with Aleki. Sylus and Maximus had gone with them, and Nyx had already ushered me into the passenger seat before climbing in behind the wheel, leaving his Warrior with no option other than to follow.

"Renita." Nyx released my name on a heavy sigh, something I'd been drawing from him a lot lately. "As a royal—"

"Nope." I cut him off, shaking my head. "We aren't having that discussion. I can't handle it." I honestly couldn't, the thought of never returning to the Coven, to my way of life… it honestly scared me more than getting caught. Nyx's grip tightened on the wheel subtly, debating how much he should push. But it was Leonardo who kicked the back of my seat with an impatient curse.

"You're gonna be a Gods damned Ocean Queen whether you can handle it or not. It's literally not your choice. So, throw your fit, and then get your shit together. The mountains couldn't be your home forever anyway."

The car screeched to a halt, Nyx whipping around to stare at Leonardo wide eyed. Both Mateo and Juan were frozen solid, I don't even think they were breathing. I stared at Leonardo in the rearview mirror, and he held my gaze unwavering even as Nyx began to chastise him under his breath. Slowly, I felt myself smiling.

"Leo..." Instantly the car fell silent again, the only sound being my clothes rustling against the seat as I turned to face him. His jaw set, the only sign of nerves as I studied him.

"I don't expect us to ever be friends," I started, his brows knitting slightly. "But if I get a choice in things, would you remain in my circle somehow? Because I'm a stubborn bitch at times and need somebody like you to set my head straight." A smirk ticked the corner of his mouth, and he lifted his chin in affirmation.

"You said it not me, majesty." I grinned, turning back around in my seat, and gesturing at the road.

"Well? Do we plan to walk from here?"

In another hour we rolled to a stop by the docks, tourists milling about in the afternoon haze which glinted off the Susquehanna. These waters would feed us into the beginnings of the Chesapeake Bay, before eventually popping us out into the North Atlantic. Already my skin crawled with the thought. I'd rarely been in saltwater; the few memories I had of it being dark in the night off the coast of Washington. Before my mind could drift to unsavory memories, my car door was yanked open, and Cillian was drawing me out and into his side.

"Finally, a form of travel that won't sicken me." I followed the direction of his extended hand, outright gawking at the sleek black yacht that was docked at the end of the pier.

"What the fuck Cillian?" I asked, unable to mask my shock. He beamed at me, the million-watt smile making my head spin.

"I splurged," he said, with a casual shrug. Aleki and the others had already headed down the pier, and he glanced back at us, eyes lingering on Cillian's arm around my shoulder and mine which had somehow wound up around his waist. I felt myself blushing, instantly stepping back to

untangle myself from him. Cillian watched me
with a bemused smile, head cocked. "Relax tesoro,
I don't bite."

"I very highly doubt that," I snapped,
turning back to the car to collect my pack, but
found that someone had once again taken it for
me. Cillian chuckled low as I practically vibrated
with annoyance.

"It's not that they don't believe you
adequate," he said, catching a strand of my hair in
his fingers, gently tugging my gaze back to him.

"They're treating me like a child," I
argued. "I know I got hurt on top of everything
else but look at me! I'm fine!" Cillian arched a
brow at my outburst, before his eyes started
slowly drifting over me. My heart felt like it was
going to burst out of my chest as his gaze lingered
on my hips, my mouth.

"They treat you with reverence," he
murmured, releasing my hair, his fingers finding
my chin. "Can you not handle affectionate
attention?"

I tensed slightly, and he felt it, smiling
wider, leaning closer. He didn't bother to mask his
inhale against my neck, his thumb stroking the
pearl stud beneath my lip, drawing it open.

"I understand," he murmured against my
skin, I could literally feel his mouth moving
against my racing pulse. "A life in hiding, not
knowing what you were. Not enough people telling

144

you that you were enough. You'll always be enough for me, tesoro."

The kiss was featherlight, but my knees buckled all the same. His hand on my lower back steadied me as he shifted, his tongue darting across my neck, tasting me. He groaned as his touch snaked up my spine, before fisting my hair. My body felt like it was on fire as he sucked gently against my pulse, melting me despite my persistent irritation. As my inward battle continued to rage, Cillian's mouth drifted lower, and a gasp tore from me when his teeth grazed the juncture of my collarbone and shoulder.

I've fucked before. That was it. It was fast, it was careless. When Aleki touched me, it was all hot and dark promises. I knew what he would give me, and wanted it desperately even if I tried to hide it.

I'd never felt stripped down with all my clothes still on though. Cillian's touch... this was a consecration.

And I didn't deserve it.

He felt the shift in me without me even needing to say a word, his mouth leaving my skin instantly. "Renita?"

"We need to go." I was already wiggling out of his grip, my nerves now tingling with anxiety instead of desire. His hand gripped my wrist, yanking me back to him.

"What did I do?" His eyes searched mine, genuine concern and care there which made one of

145

my carefully built walls begin to crack.
Everything in me was wailing now. My magic, my
blood, the heartbeat between my legs. This was
beyond dangerous, this could kill us both. But
Gods, I was tempted.

"Nothing." My voice was perfectly calm,
my ability to lie unfettered. An ability I need now
more than ever. "Let's join the others. And now
that I have cell service, I would like to call my
aunt. I assume I'll have my own room aboard that
eccentric thing?"

His nod was stiff, confusion and hurt
rolling off him in waves but I ignored it. His
attachment to me wasn't my problem, nor was
Aleki's. I was a woman, a powerful woman, a royal
woman. They were tempted, naturally. And I
would no longer fault myself for my own
inappropriate thoughts.

However, I was here to protect my Coven.
It was my duty as a Mer to protect my King. But
no matter how far I let myself slip within this
bubble in time, I could not allow myself to freefall.
Royal or not, the Sea would not have me for long.

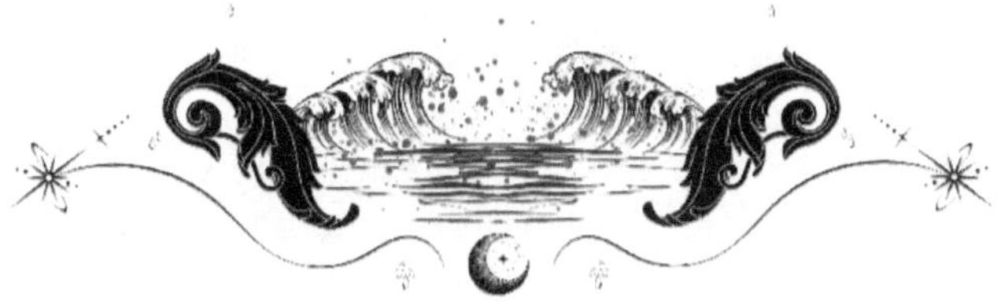

18

Cillian

The yacht moved slowly, designed for open bodies of water, not these rocky curves. I didn't bother telling Renita about the extra precautions I took, our glamour cloaking the yacht, leaving us mostly unseen except by those with an exceptional third eye. I doubted any reassurances I gave her would hit their intended mark.

Alek also, sensing the shift in her, gave her a wide berth. I replayed the other night, when that thing attacked us, in my mind over and over. She hadn't so much as paused before taking on the beast, the command in her voice forcing even me to pause. Perhaps she felt guilty— I doubt she ever used her glamour to that extent before.

It had been... thrilling for me. No matter how brief, I couldn't have moved even if I wanted to. That lack of control in her hands... Part of me believed she didn't realize she was capable of that. But another part, a louder part, had begun pushing against the admiration.

She was wild and fierce, that we all knew. But… she hadn't fought in the way of defense. It was more vicious, the bloodshed more intentional. Now, I'm not going to sit here and pretend I'm an expert on how to handle a cryptid, but I was getting pretty familiar with reading Renita, and patterns were beginning to emerge.

The night the Sirens attacked us at her home she hadn't fought like a Manipulative. She fought like a Warrior, each attack aimed to be a death blow if she could force it, rather than a deterrence. The way she held an icy blade to my throat, her tracking and hunting of the buck, and now that… monster. Even the weapon she bothered to use against it was minimalist compared to what she did with her bare hands. From the glimpses of the fight I saw between flashes of lightning, she was even tearing it apart with her teeth. She hadn't raised a drop of water magic against it that I saw, unless I counted the sudden raging storm. Something was stirring in her, a violence which she kept buried deep within herself, and I wanted to expose it.

I understood her retreating from me once that fight alerted us to what she actually was. Knowing her, she probably felt more trapped than ever, and me running my mouth about ruling side by side hadn't helped matters. But I didn't understand her retreating from my men.

By my instruction, they stopped coddling her. The air of respect was still there, but they went back to being conversational and light. She wasn't raised in a world that would have revered her simply for the shade of her scales; she would need time to adjust, and not on a timeline I would allow any of them to dictate.

Yet, she remained holed up in her suite, a floor beneath mine. Not even Juan or Mateo could coax her out, though by now they have taken shifts in delivering meals and watching over her door at night. Nyx had grown increasingly bitter, having taken a liking to her which he rarely afforded others.

My obsession with her had only grown as the days passed. If Alek hadn't coaxed me to bed, or Maximus hadn't dragged me out of my room to train, I would be pacing. Ears straining for any sound below. On the occasion I let myself out to stretch, I'd be watching her window from the river. I knew when she ate, when she showered, and soon, when she snuck out.

Three am, every night. The land dwellers Witching Hour, of course. Mer or no, her soul was tied to her sister's practice. It just made my curiosity grow even more. Enough so that one night I didn't simply listen for her to sneak out her bathroom window. Didn't simply watch the flash of her scales through the dark waters as she rounded the boat. I followed her.

Not in the water, it was too risky. Too open. Instead, like a stalker, I tiptoed my way along the gangway, pausing in the shadows. She was just swimming, clinging to any ounce of privacy she could. So why couldn't I shake the feeling that something bigger was going on?

I debated with myself for a minute, before a ragged curse left my lips and I dove in. It took all of two seconds for her to be upon me, one clawed hand poised behind her to strike, but her eyes were widened in surprise seeing me. My tail brushed hers under the water, slow and lazy, and she snapped away, regaining her distance.

"What the fuck Cillian?" Her outrage rang in my ears as I surfaced a few feet away. I shrugged, eyes drifting to the yacht which continued to float downriver.

"Shockingly, I also prefer to swim in private." I lowered my voice. "We tend to attract unnecessary attention otherwise, don't we?"

I stretch out on the water's surface, floating on my back to purposely allow her to get a good look at my tail. My eyes had drifted to the stars above, studying the unfamiliar constellations. Though I was born in the Caribbean Sea, as soon as I was large enough to survive, I had been sent to live at the edge of the Artic Circle. My scales refracted light like shards of ice, or fresh fallen snow. It was safer for me to blend in there before I learned how to adjust their shade or withhold shifting altogether.

The first touch of her fingertips had my tail flick instinctively, heart leaping into my throat. Besides my mother and Alek, no one had dared to touch me when I shifted, let alone my tail itself. I actually had to fight the urge to squirm as her fingers trailed over the iridescent crests of my dorsal fins. They started at my hips, rippling on the current, before tapering off into shorter points down the sides of my tail.

"Aleki said his tail mimic's a tiger shark." Her voice drifting off the water was as soft as her touch. "Do you all mimic different ocean creatures."

"No. Most just mimic the environments in which we were born." I try to steer the subject, fascinate her with our lineage. "Typically, the strength of one's magic is what dictates just how detailed their tail is."

"Which fish do you mimic?" She asks, not letting it go. I sigh, my eyes shutting.

"A butterfly fish." There's a full moments pause, before her laughter is ricocheting off the water and into the night. I toss an arm across my face, feeling my skin heating in a blush.

"No, I can see it though," she finally speaks, gathering her wits. "Your fins have similar dark spots which pattern many of the butterflies living in the mountains. Identical and eye catching to distract predators away from your most vital areas. Not to mention, you are kind of delicate." With that I sat up, sinking my tail beneath the surface and grabbing her hand.

"For a woman who doesn't wish to be worshipped for her literal place in our world, you have a lot of nerve calling me delicate." Though my tone was scathing, she just grinned.

"You're proving me right. Look at you, your delicate little ego all puffed up and in my

151

face." I released an annoyed groan, blushing deeper. Her free hand rose from the water to cup my cheek, and I froze. "And this face of yours," she murmurs. "Elegant and soft, like a high fae."

I didn't know what a high fae was, but I loved the way she was looking at me. As the thought struck my mind it was like she finally realized our position, pulling her hand away from me again. I sighed heavily, growing tired of this.

"Renita—"

"Stop." The word was damn near a plea, and I grit my teeth.

"Stop what?" I growled, yanking her towards me through the water. Her tail smacked mine and I grinned, looping an arm around her hips. "Stop what?" I repeated, gentler this time. "Making you feel? Making you crave? Tempting you to break whatever rules you've written for yourself?" I lowered my chin so my mouth could graze her neck, a tremor shaking through her and I paused.

"I will not kid myself into believing you're here because you want to be. I know it's out of duty, to both our world and your Coven. However," I groaned as her nails dug into my arms, and I responded by rolling my tongue over her racing pulse. "You came on my boyfriend's tongue. And based on your body language, you've been fighting the urge to ask to cum on mine."

"I'm here to help your dumbass not die on your trip back to the sea!" She snaps, nails raking from my shoulders to my elbows, and this time I bite the crook of her neck. A hushed gasp fell from her lips, and I smirked against her wet skin.

"You've been more than just helpful in that area," I agree, pulling back to grin up at her. "But I'm here to relieve you of all the pent-up stress I've been causing you, if you'll let me." Her tail smacked against mine, but we both knew if she wanted out of my grip, she'd be out.

I ducked under the water, mouth slowly trailing kisses between her collarbones to finally land my tongue on one of her peaked nipples. Her fingers fisted my hair as my touch slid south from her ribs to her hips, mapping where skin turned to scale. The fact that she was letting me have her like this was almost enough to push me over the edge right there, but I was determined to savor her.

My mouth left her nipple swollen and I immediately migrated to the other. This time, I sank my teeth into the soft underside, sucking gently. My fingers traced her navel, feeling her heart pounding beneath my touch. Before I lost my shit and claimed her right there, I forced myself to surface. She looked nearly as desperate as I was, and the way her lips were parted made me curse under my breath.

"Shift," I demanded, voice hoarse. Her brows furrowed so I slid my hand behind her, fingers drifting against the inconspicuous slit in her scales beneath her arched dorsal fin which curved over her rear. "Unless you're curious about

153

how to do it our way, shift. I'm at my breaking
point with you."

A satisfied groan left my lips when she
listened, now treading water with slow kicks of
her legs. She wouldn't have to do that for long.

I dove back beneath the surface, wrapping
her legs around my head, my tongue sinking
between the soft folds of her sex. Her hips bucked
against my face when I nipped her clit, her cry
echoing down through the water to me. I didn't
stop for anything. Not when her moans turned to
screams. Not when the current pushed us to
shore. If anything, that was better, her on her
back writhing beneath me, the water splashing as
she gave into her ecstasy. I drank every last drop
of it from her before rising over her body, cupping
her cheeks.

"Please let me have you," I begged, scales
shifting to skin as I hovered over her. The water
dripping off me rolled over her curves, her chest
heaving for breath, eyes heavy and unfocused.
"Tesoro please, I will not keep going unless you—"

"Don't stop." Her words were low but gave
me all the permission I needed.

I gasped outright as I eased myself into
her tight channel. Then she arched beneath me,
the angle causing me to bottom out inside her in
half a second. She whined, and the ragged moan
which left me had her eyes going dark. Her legs
looped around my waist as I drew back, yanking
me back in and forcing another moan from me.

"Wow," she breathed, and my nerves flared to life, embarrassed now as she studied my reactions. But she wasn't mocking me, if anything, she looked more turned on. She lifted her hips, teasing my length in her walls, making me tremble. "Roll over Cillian," she urged, determination and hunger in her eyes.

I did, my hands gripping her hips tightly, but my grip did nothing to stop her from moving. Now I was the one moaning out into the dark, my voice cracking as she rolled her hips in a way that stole my breath. Desperately I thrust up to meet her, needing to be deeper, faster. I was rewarded when she cried out, the sound thick with uncontrolled glamour, like absinthe to my nervous system.

I lost myself, forcing her hips flush to mine as I drilled into her from below. Her muscles went taught as she came, walls clenching me tightly, milking me for all I was worth.

Our ragged breaths filled the night air, her thighs trembling where they lay parted over my hips. I ground my teeth as I gently lifted her off, my body screaming to keep her close, but my soul wanting to comfort her however she needed.

We were still half in the water, and I urged her lower, my hand slipping between her thighs to clean her gently. She shivered against each brush of my fingers even though I was being careful. The exchange was wordless, but not uncomfortable. She shifted back first, the metallic silver of her scales glittering under the stars.

I took in the details. How the small, hooked fins on her spine trailed to the large dorsal. The smattering of grey scales against her hips, like a summer storm. She gleamed in the night, like she herself was a star. I desperately wanted to ask where she was from, but with her finally calm and content in my presence, I barely dared to breathe.

We swam back to the ship in silence, shifting back to climb up the gangway. When we reached her doorway, I thought she would pause. I even dared to imagine a kiss, but all I received was a quick glance over her shoulder before the lock quietly turned. I blinked, my brain trying to process what just happened. And then a low whistle sounded from down the hall.

"Damn Cillian." Alek's voice reached me, warm and abating. I bristled anyways, guilt rolling through me.

"Alek—"

"Oh stop." His arms circled my bare waist, pulling me against him. The move instantly reassured me of everything. Her dismissal, my actions, whatever the fuck was happening between us or not. "My only concern is that I do not lose you completely." His voice was hushed in my ear, a gentle kiss just above it.

"Never." I promised, leaning back into him.

"Let's get you to bed, my King." It was my turn to scoff this time, but still I let him lead me

back to my room, refusing to sleep without him in
my arms.

19

Renita

I could scream and curse myself to the depths and back for my lack of self-restraint. First of all, I had almost killed him when he followed me. I truly hadn't realized it was him, not until his eyes flashed purple in the dark. And the fool! He didn't even look surprised by my attack, was already smiling even, completely unaware of what I had been doing and the danger he was in.

But it was guilt that was plaguing me more. For the majority of the night I had tossed and turned, my rushing thoughts on Aleki. Sure, I'd let him touch me, but Cillian had seen it— and at this point I highly suspected that Aleki had intended him to. This was different. I had snuck away in the middle of the night with his boyfriend and… gods, I didn't even try to glamour Cillian away.

My urges have been getting worse recently. The fluctuation of my power was growing unsteady and unpredictable. After only two days on the river, I had begun to salivate. It was the peak of summer now, so the waters were flooded with boats and floaters during the day. The number of scents and sounds, the pulsing enticement of a human's blood on my tongue, was beginning to terrify me.

The only way to keep it wrangled was shifting as often as possible now, tracking and killing whatever I could. I tried to go without, but knew I was going to fail. And I would rather hate myself for gutting fish with my teeth than finally snapping and making a true kill with the audience of the Mer.

They had been prickly, clearly unhappy with the distance I'd been putting between us. I understood that to them it had to feel unnatural, but it was for their own safety. We needed to get to the sea. I needed to be filled in on the Siren problem because yes, now I was beginning to think that as one of them I could solve it. If they clung to any sense of decorum, one of their own being a royal would have to carry some weight, right? And then go the fuck home before my fangs wound up in someone's throat.

And Cillian, the idiot! He was going to be King but had zero awareness of danger. I had to think fast before he smelled the blood in the water, had to give my body something in order to avoid it being his blood. And his eagerness made every urge I had even more overwhelming. I'd never been with a man who was so into it, so giving, so *verbal*. The primal parts of me that were beating at their cages absolutely reveled in the way he let me take over, coming undone beneath me like the most natural thing in the world.

So. Fucking. Dangerous.

"Top of the morning to ya, little predator." I was dragged from my thoughts by Aleki's cheerful shout. My gaze drifted from the horizon to find him lounging in a pool floaty secured to the yacht with a mooring line. A neon pink flamingo pool floaty.

"Where did that come from?" I asked, trying not to let the guilt and anxiety creep into my voice. I sank back into my coffee, the mug warm against my lips. Like a pathetic shield.

"It was in one of the storge bunks." He was sitting cross legged, holding a ridiculously bright blue drink in hand, complete with a plastic green spiral straw and matching mini umbrella poked through a cheery.

"It's 7am," I murmured. He smirked.

"I'm on vacation."

"Is that what you're calling this?" I asked, already feeling my tension ease. There was no way Cillian had kept our late-night rendezvous a secret, and Aleki didn't seem the type of man to fake emotions. If he was upset, surely, he would tell me. I realized now that we actually hadn't seen or spoken to each other since we boarded a week ago. Hadn't been alone with him since we—

"Cillian's got you in quite a spin, doesn't he?" Instantly heat rushed to my face and I heard him chuckle. "He'd done the same to me. Trust me, once you get a taste of that, there's no letting him go."

"Watch me." My tone was sharp, my glare severe despite the irritating blush on my skin. Aleki just smiled wider, head tilting like this was a challenge. In half a beat he was out of the floaty, the powerful muscles in his arms hoisting himself over the rail to cage me in.

I refused to give him the satisfaction of reacting, even when his weight settled against my back. I took another sip of coffee, eyes glued to the red sun, its rays reflecting off the gentle waves in the water.

"Why?" The simple curiosity of his question caught me off guard, having me ask before I could think better of it.

"Why what?"

"Why aren't you clarifying anything?"

If my braincells could explode, I'm certain a few just did. I abandoned my coffee on the rail, turning to face him, having to crane my neck to meet his eyes. He was assessing me, an element of distrust in his gaze for the first time, and I bristled.

"You were hiding in a town full of witches," he murmured, fingers absently reaching out to play with the end of one of my curls. "Lied to us when we first arrived. Lied about what you were when we finally realized you were a Mer."

"I didn't lie," I argued. His hand surged upwards to the nape of my neck, yanking my hair to tilt my head back, silencing me.

"You weren't honest, little predator." Another stone dropped in my stomach, the pit of guilt deepening. "Why lie to us so much? Why keep so many secrets? And why give both Cillian and I that desperately needy look you're giving me right now?"

My mouth was dry, but I forced a swallow. His eyes locked on my throat, tracking the move. A predator indeed.

"I know nothing of your world, and frankly, don't know if I want to live in it." The words made a wounded look cross his features, his grip falling from me.

"Why not? It's where you belong. Even the Gods—"

"The Gods made a mistake!" His brows furrowed at my shout, hands gingerly resting on my elbows, holding me steady. I hadn't even realized I'd begun shaking. Once I started, the words just kept coming.

"I'm not supposed to be here. I'm meant to be in the woods, the mountains, finding refuge in magic. Not the sea. I was abandoned by it long ago. The Gods did not listen to my cries. They ignored my pleas to spare my mother. And I do blame the Mer for what happened to her." My hand fisted his shirt, a hiss leaving him as my claws tore the fabric and his skin.

"If not for your stupid laws the Sirens would have no reason to attack! She would be alive if you didn't create yourselves an enemy out of fear. One that's angry enough to—"

"Renita." My mouth snapped shut at Cillian's voice, my entire body freezing. He wasn't alone, all of them were standing up the deck, staring at me wide eyed. His eyes were glowing violet, a command deepening his voice. "Let him go."

Blood stained the front of Aleki's shirt, and I kept my mouth firmly shut, feeling the sharpened points of my teeth pressing against my lips. Cillian approached us slowly, surprising me by not tending to Aleki and instead cupping my cheek, tilting my head this way and that.

"You can fight it all you wish, but you know you belong in the sea. Your body knows this, as does your soul. It's only your stubbornness in your way." I growled, the sound menacing enough to make both Maximus and Leonardo step forwards, but Aleki echoed the sound, halting them instantly. I glanced at him, confused, but he offered nothing. Cillian drew my attention back to him with a finger under my chin, thumb on my pearl again.

"We will never be able to sympathize with the extent of what's been taken from you, unless you allow us to."

"I don't want your sympathy."

"I don't care." His eyes flashed again, wholly replacing Aleki in front of me until it was him crowding me against the rail. "I will never lock you under the sea, but I will also not allow you to continue to hide. Surely, even before we stumbled into your life, you knew you would return to the water eventually?"

My voice caught in my throat, a strangled sound leaving me. I'd always felt the pull. Never talked about it. Never dared acknowledge it. The river was enough. It had to be, after everything that was done.

Cillian's grip on my chin tightened, a sharp prick from the angle my piercing was in, and I glared at him with everything I had. A huff of annoyance left him, and then he did something I never thought he would do. I was suddenly dangling upside down from his shoulder, his arm hooked around the back of my knees to keep me in place.

"You spoiled rotten bastard!" I screeched, fists pounding his back, but he didn't so much as flinch. He ignored my curses as he carried me, kicking and screaming to the back of the yacht; the rest of them following warily. Instead of setting me down, I was yanked roughly from his shoulder and then chucked into the open air.

The water drowned my curses as I plunged in, the shock of what he just did overpowering my grip on my self-control. I shifted with a brilliant flash of silver, the sounds of the others diving into the river surrounding me making every one of my defenses rise.

The murky water seemed to glow slightly, a pulsing viridian light glinting off their scales, making them shine almost like mine. A flash of red had me placing Aleki moments before a blinding burst of white had me shielding my eyes.

"Open your mouth." It was Aleki's voice but Cillian's hands on me, his thumb forcing itself between my teeth, pressing down on my tongue. I coughed as the water flowed in, my tail whipping desperately but I was pinned between them.

Typically, I would hold my breath. I could for hours at a time. It had been well over a decade since my chest was flooded, and the stretch to accommodate the gallons being forced down my throat burned more than I thought it would. I bit down with my teeth, Cillian cursing but not removing his thumb from my mouth until my breaths had calmed, my body adjusting, relaxing against my will.

"So many secrets," he growled, now purposely trailing his thumb over my fangs, marveling at them when he should be screaming.

"A barracuda is fitting for you, my Queen," Aleki purred in my ear.

The others were circling us, gentle clicks and whines echoing through the water like bells and horns. Cillian's eyes were gleaming, the purple iris's reflecting the green glow of the water around us. I practically spit his thumb out of my mouth when his grip loosened.

"Why the fuck does it taste like this?" My question took even me by surprise, neither of the men caging me in seeming to have a response.

"It's brackish water." Our eyes snapped to Nyx who I hadn't even seen approaching. His inky tail was near invisible in this water, and the warm tones of his skin blended in with the sandy riverbed. "I don't much like the taste of it either, but it'll clear up in a few miles when we reach the bay."

Bay. Ice coated my nerves, and Aleki instantly drew me back into his chest.

"Be calm, Renita. You're safe."

Everything in me was screaming to flee, tears streaming down my face under the water in a rush. Mateo had materialized beside Cillian, concern etching his features.

Beyond my power I was drawn back to that cliffside. The gentle hum of the river was replaced by the screaming of lightning. The crashing of waves, foaming around the body far below. And I fell, because I jumped. I'd choose my mother's fate before I let the Mer take me.

"Tesoro..."

"That's not gonna work." It was Leonardo's voice which dragged me back. Aleki's weight against me disappeared, and suddenly I was no longer falling, I was being dragged upwards. My head broke the surface and I cried out, water streaming from my nose and mouth. Leonardo's grip on the back of my neck was tight, forcing me to face ahead.

"Just look," he demanded, voice low. I blinked the water from my eyes, a silent sob shaking me as my gaze focused. Waves. Sand. Open... nothing but the water, and the horizon.

"You ordered me to stay by your side, so that when you pulled shit like this, someone wouldn't let you," he reminded me, finally releasing his hold on me with a soft push forwards, closer to deeper waters.

"I-... I'm..." I was still crying, unable to formulate a word let alone a sentence. One by one they surfaced, Mateo still looking worried, but Juan made him keep his distance. Nyx and Leonardo both looked annoyed, Maximus bored, and Sylus was muttering in his ear clearly anxious. Aleki's playful demeanor was for once absent, replaced by that cool assessment again. And Cillian gave me the same look he did in the diner. Shocked, pleased, and wanting.

The glow to the water had finally begun to dull, pulling back to me, I realized. My skin still held that vibrant hue, and instinctively I knew my eyes were glowing in similar fashion to how Cillian's could. How a royals would.

"The forest was your sanctuary," he said,
his earlier anger gone, replaced by cold resolution.
"But this is your home. Your birthright. Take it."

20

Renita

I couldn't fib myself into wanting to leave the water. Everything around me had begun to blur and pulse. The riverbed, the schools of fish, the kelp growing up towards the sun. Never before had I felt cramped in the river or lake until now, flying through the bay the same way I had watched the birds soaring over the mountain peaks in the early morning.

None of them stopped me when I took off, only Nyx following me against Leonardo's protests. Freedom felt terrifying.

I felt what he'd meant as the water shifted, the sharp contrast smoothing to the bitter kiss of salt. I was too young to remember what this water felt like on my tongue, on my scales, but if it was anything close to this, I don't know how my mother convinced me to leave it.

Deep water called to me, the murkiness of the river giving way to the ancient blues and greys of the bay floor. The Chesapeake was cold even in the dead of summer, the chill from the North Atlantic seeping into her waters. I didn't care though. I was busy with following the scrabbled paths of horseshoe crabs on the shadowy floor, the sunlight blurring to an incandescent this deep. Oysters tumbled over one another as schools of fish burst by, disturbing the relative calm in the belly of the bay. I felt like anchoring myself here, becoming a buoy to the tide and never surfacing again.

"I wish you could see your face," Nyx commented, the powerful whips of his midnight tail allowing him to keep up with me easily.

"You should have stayed with the others." I didn't even care he was teasing me, this bliss made everything worth it. He snorted, as if my comment was the dumbest I could have made.

"Apologies my Queen, but I'd prefer to keep eyes on you and your… unpredictable tendencies." I opened my mouth, a defensive retort on the verge of spilling but his laughter cut me off. "Besides, Leonardo is close by. He wouldn't let me risk myself, even for you."

Anxiety that I hadn't been aware of until then settled instantly knowing that. I didn't argue further, and we swam in comfortable silence as the channel narrowed, the water eddying beyond the curve of Norfolk, and spilling into the open ocean. I felt myself hesitating there, my body locking up, clinging to the security which I had imprinted on the land for the majority of my life.

"Perhaps it would be best to return?" Nyx offered, sensing my warring desires. I only nodded, following him towards the darkening surface as night crept over the heavens. I was stunned to realize we had spent the entire day down here— it hadn't felt longer than an hour or two to me.

"So where are we going?" I asked once we'd surfaced and the water stopped pouring from my mouth. Nyx hovered near the stern of the yacht, one hand gripping the ladder and his other extended to me.

"Our party comes from many different waters," he says, holding me steady and keeping his gaze on the horizon as I shift. "I hail from the Yellow Sea, the others come scattered from Caribbean and Pacific waters. The current King," his tone sharpened subtly, but I didn't miss it. "He resides in the Spanish Isle's, which is where we intend to return with you."

I pursed my lips, disliking the way he described it, but didn't push for now. Nyx's loyalties were clear— this whole groups was. I would trust them as much as I could, considering the circumstance, but...

"When he learns of what I am, I'm stuck, aren't I?" I ask, hauling myself up onto the deck, grabbing one of the towels from the pile and wrapping it around myself.

"If he learns, yes." Nyx hoists himself out of the water, rolling himself until his tail fully emerged to drip-dry on the deck. I felt my breath catch, a faint spark of hope through my rising fear.

"What do you mean if?"

Nyx stretches his arms, lacing his fingers behind his head and relaxing back. He looked like Maria's cat, sunning himself in the waning dusk.

"Power is not handed down, it's bestowed. You know that." His voice was low, calm. "I have zero intention of alerting the King of any information that does not pertain his safety. You are a royal. I exist to serve you as equally as I exist to serve him."

"You," I felt like I was choking on the words in my shock. "You would keep it a secret?" That had a smile curving his lips for a moment.

"As far as we are concerned, you're a Mer cursed to live without a tail. Right?"

I was stunned into silence, both taken aback and extremely grateful. If they were willing to keep that part of my identity a secret, that would make this whole affair so much easier. I could do my duty as the Mers culture demanded, supporting the future King until the threat of the Sirens was subdued and after that... well, I can't imagine any royal would require a Mer without a tail to remain at court. I'd be free.

A knot of worry interrupted the rush of my relief, as I realized how difficult pulling this off would be. Just being in the sea for a day had rocked my entire system. I doubted I would have the control to not shift for the duration of my appearance at court, and didn't know if I would have any private accommodations secure enough to give myself the relief. And that risk was far smaller than my Siren tendencies.

I would not be able to hunt, to feed properly. The urges which I had stupidly been allowing myself to indulge in throughout the past few weeks would doom me, no matter what color my scales were. Not to mention the risk my secret now posed to Cillian and his men if they were caught harboring and endorsing me. In the short time I had been traveling with them, I had grown attached to each of them in their own way. Regardless of how they felt about me, regardless if I could find any acceptance for what I was as a whole, this small group had begun unravelling me. And now my true nature was a tangible threat to us all.

"Enjoy your swim, little predator?" Aleki's voice startles me from my racing thoughts, and I find him leaning on the railing at the top of the stairs. Rather than eyeing me up like I'm his next meal, his gaze is soft. His gentle smile catches me staring. "Relief looks good on you."

I roll my eyes, holding my towel tighter as I stand and finally march up the stairs. Nyx didn't budge. Frankly, he looks like he's fallen asleep right there, and I was intent to let him after making him chase me around all day like a toddler with sudden freedom in the park.

"It was refreshing," I murmur as I slide past Aleki, making him chuckle.

"Do you know where we are headed?" He asks, following at what I'm sure he thought was a respectful distance.

"Nyx filled me in." I didn't turn, following the narrow halls back to my room. I needed clothes. And food. I haven't eaten anything since that fish I shredded with my bare teeth.

"The trip will be far shorter than you might expect," Aleki said, stopping a few feet back from my door. "There's a cruise leaving for Spain tomorrow which we've already secured rooms for. We'll arrive in less than a week, letting the ship do the hard part rather than draining our magic by pushing this fancy, yet ultimately useless yacht to its limits." He pauses, and I can damn near feel the smirk curving his mouth as I open my door. "Maybe I'll take you dancing one night. Would you like that?"

I actually hesitate; the door halfway shut between us as I considered his offer. It would be nice, something normal in the midst of all of this. But I didn't know what accepting would imply. As if reading my thoughts he took half a step closer, his tone more controlled than before.

"I would very much enjoy getting to spend time in just your company, but I wouldn't overstep if your desires have changed."

"Why do you word it like that?" I grumble, feeling my cheeks heat with a blush. He cocks his head.

"What? Desire?" He grins. "That's what it is, isn't it? It's nothing to be shameful about." At my silence his eyes narrow, assessing me just like he did when he found me at the lake.

"...I think I understand the problem," he finally says, his body filling the doorway now. "Your time on land, in such a controlled and stressful environment has put a few, shall we say, narrow ideas in your head. You're struggling with the fact you're intrigued by each of us."

He doesn't have to name him. We both know he's talking about Cillian. Suddenly my chin is gripped, my gaze yanked upwards until I'm forced to meet his heated gaze.

"Mer live for a long time, Renita." I shivered when my name left his tongue, and he tracked it, his hand sliding to my neck, gripping gently.

"The others may intend to let you do whatever you want because of your newfound authority. But as you have seen with my interactions with the King, I pursue relentlessly unless it is something that is truly unwanted. And Cillian himself is going to fight like hell to keep you. This will be at your pace, my Queen, but you will not be able to avoid it forever." Slowly, his smile turned wolfish. I tasted the first hint of my surrender, not wanting to move and risk breaking whatever spell he had me under.

"And while we're on the topic," he murmured, slowly leaning closer. His grip on my neck tightened a degree, making heat pool between my legs almost instantly. Then his mouth brushed my jaw, openly breathing me in as he whispered,

"Rest assured: you'll get to experience the full extent of whatever pretty little thoughts you've seemed desperate to hide from us. Hatred, disdain, whatever you want to call it to make yourself feel better. Those things don't give off the sweet perfume clinging to you right now."

He left me like that, standing in my doorway only half aware of myself. I could still feel his fingers against my pulse, the blood rushing so fast I could hear it roaring in my ears. Slowly, I closed my door, hunger forgotten as I fell limply to my bed. I craved sleep now more than ever, if only to obliterate the rising swell of wanting in my veins.

21

Renita

I have no idea what they did with the yacht. Juan and Mateo had flanked me the moment I'd left my room and ushered me straight to the boardwalk. They'd insisted the few extra jeans and T-shirts in my bag would not suffice for the trip ahead, and I didn't have the energy to argue against the truth.

Despite protesting vehemently, a golden credit card which I highly suspected was Cillian's was forced into my hands. I had money from the Coven, but when Mateo offered my only other option as them glamouring the shopkeepers to allow me to take whatever I wanted, I quickly agreed to use the card without more of a fuss. Though there were still a handful of murmured comments I hurled when their backs were turned.

For about two hours I was paraded through every shop that was open that early. Only

after I'd procured four new pairs of shoes, two
very unnecessary bikinis, and several new outfits,
was I allowed to break free from the shopping
spree and flee to the comforts of a small café.

By that time, it was bustling, so the three
of us wound up sharing a small corner table by
the window. The space was entirely too small for
the two of them, packed together like sardines in
the booth, but they didn't voice a complaint.
Silently I nursed my iced coffee, nausea working
its way in so I could only poke at the sugary pile of
French toast on my plate. Reality about what I
was going to need to face was beginning to set in.
A whole world I had been shielded from, a part to
play that I was already struggling with and I
wasn't even on the mainstage yet.

"Tesoro?" I started at the sound of
Cillian's voice. My head whipped up when I felt
his weight against the back of my chair as he
squeezed himself into our corner, using my
shoulders as leverage to ease himself back against
the wall. The touch made a chill run down my
spine, and mentally I cursed Aleki for the
encouragements I didn't want nor need. Cillian
though just squeezed gently, in a way I'm sure he
meant as comforting since he was oblivious to the
tandem wreaking havoc through me. "Did you find
everything you were looking for?"

"Considering it was against my will, I
found more than necessary," I grumbled, already
working his card out of my wallet to hand back to
him. He somehow leaned even closer, nearly
curling over me to ease the card back into my

wallet. "Cillian," I started, already feeling guilty enough but he cut me off.

"You don't have to use it, but there's no reason to return it. Its an account I opened years ago and hadn't had the need for until now."

I felt myself frowning deeper, twisting in my seat to face him. He remained craned over me, our faces closer than necessary. Again, I chastised my stupid body. His breath on my cheek should do nothing. My heart shouldn't be galloping. This was a man that would sooner kill me than—

"Can I attempt to interrupt whatever argument you're surely cooking up?" He asked, eyes flashing violet briefly and I swore he did it on purpose just to screw with me.

"... Sure." I don't know why I agreed. Maybe it was a fleeting sense of curiosity which I shouldn't harbor. Maybe it was my competitive nature, rising to the playful challenge in his tone. Either way, I lost the moment I caved.

He leaned even closer, his lips brushing my ear, his hand sliding to my thigh. Sparks flew through my nervous system, my body remembering every intimate detail about what he could do. And based on the pleased groan he tried to keep low in his throat, he was probably experiencing a similar swell of... desire. Damn it, Aleki. Cillian cleared his throat, voice rough.

"That card is attached to only one account. It's not my wealth, so you don't owe me anything. I opened it, depositing what you would probably describe as a disgustingly high fortune into it, with the intention of only allowing my future Queen to use it." His lips pecked the soft spot beneath my ear as I squirmed, facing forwards in my seat again.

His future Queen. It wasn't the first time he'd said it, but it was the first time I realized how serious he was. My palms began to sweat, knowing I needed to shut this down before we got to Spain, before I could do anything to permanently mess his future up. And yet everything in my body was screaming against it. Unraveled wasn't the right word anymore. It wasn't large enough to describe how in just a few short weeks these men had taken my world and made it spin on a new axis.

"I'm not going with you as a Queen," I said, my voice too light, too breathy. His hand squeezed my thigh tighter in response, like he was trying to call me on my bullshit. Juan and Mateo had disappeared, both a relief from further embarrassment, but also an annoyance as I was left alone to barely tread water.

"Why?" He sounded far more hurt than I expected. I didn't turn, knowing I wouldn't be able to bear the look on his face. I took a slow, steadying breath, trying to calm my racing heart.

"Yes. I feel things for you that I don't want to feel." The intensity of his gaze on me multiplied at the admission, but I pressed on.

"I feel as equally confused and annoyed by Aleki. The combination of that is already bordering on too much, so how can you expect me to take the throne of world I don't know?" I was wringing my hands now, reciting the original plan like it was a prayer that could save me.

"I came with you to protect my home, and to fulfill my duty as a Mer. Protect the King from the threat. And then be free to go back to my life."

"Your duty as a Mer is to rule." His tone had sharpened slightly, disbelief and annoyance blending. "You were chosen for that. Blessed. You can't just reject it."

"Watch me." I tilted my head back again as he straightened, resting it against his abdomen. He was glaring down at me now, and it was hot. Cillian angry was a temptation in and of itself, but I couldn't give in again.

At this point, alone in my head I could acknowledge it wasn't about me. My distance and rejections had little to do with my feelings on the Mer, or my stance on him and Aleki. By now, my defiance and avoidance had wholly shifted for their safety. I was a Siren, the creature which was their greatest threat. I needed to hold myself accountable, keep my distance, and curb my urges. It was the only way to keep them all safe from their own world.

"Nyx made it clear that the others would keep my secret, only revealing what I allowed." Cillian's nostril's flared, his temper continuing to rise and I grinned. "Oh please. I'm a royal, right? It's only natural they would listen to my command."

Suddenly both his hands were on my hips, and a bubble of silence descended over us, masking us from the rest of the café.

"You really are the most vexing woman I've ever met," he growled, eyes roaming me freely. "Refusing your own throne, yet puppeteering its advantages better than most."

"Well..." My voice shook, adrenaline flooding me as I continued to push, walking a tightrope of giving in and holding back. "Apparently that's your taste in women. Can't hold me accountable for something you have newly discovered."

His eyes went wholly violet, and the eager, wanting part of me which I'd buried broke free. My hand slid over my thigh, caressing where his touch had been. Then trailed higher. He tracked the movement, jaw locked. But before I could touch myself, he shattered the spell around us.

His hands flew off of me as if I'd burned him, and he damn near sprinted out of the space behind my chair. Juan and Mateo immediately surfaced from the counter, and I abandoned my plate, refusing to even acknowledge what I'd almost instigated.

"It's time to board." His voice was grating, angry, desperate and making my mouth water. "We might be able to glamour the whole staff, but that cruise will still leave with or without us."

I was tense as I watched him walk away, heart and mind rushing in synch. Stupid. I was so fucking stupid and careless.

"You heard him," I grumbled to the twins. As I looped the plastic handles of my bags through my arms, I couldn't help but wonder now who was actually in the most danger. Them, or me.

I thought I'd be overwhelmed by the cruise. Though I lived in a tourist town, we had a reliable off season, and things ran on routine. A cruise ship was a thousand people squashed together, with a million different scents and sounds 24/7. Juan stuck close to my side as we boarded, but shockingly, I found the chaos of it all soothing. So soothing in fact that I didn't even unpack, just chucked my stuff in my suite and immediately disappeared into the throng of people.

It was the first time since leaving Sashomik that I hadn't been with one of the Mer. Armed with a neon orange drink with a pink plastic twisty straw in hand, I set out to explore the ship on my own.

It was easy to find the areas to avoid. The smokers lounge reeked despite the attempts to keep the air fresh. And the kids' zone was loud and stinky enough to create a naturally wide berth. The open pools up on the deck were nice, depending on the time of day. I grabbed a flyer for the party schedules in effort to mitigate the amount of people around when I took the future opportunity to soak.

For once, I found myself envying the Mer, but my pride would not allow me to seek one of them out and ask how to glamour my tail away. I'd just wait till everyone was asleep, because the little chain with a 'closed' sign wouldn't be keeping me out of the water at the witching hour.

Now the restaurants, I was practically living in those. Plus, it gave me an excuse to wear all the new clothes I was forced to buy as well. Sylus and Maximus often joined me to eat. They shared stories of all the places they'd travelled over the two centuries they knew one another, Sylus doing most of the talking with the occasional nod or correction from Maximus. It struck me in those moments just how young I was in their world. It made the group's actions, and tendencies to hover, feel a bit less oppressive than they initially did.

Every so often someone would swing by my room to check on me, or just so happen to appear wherever I was, enjoying the entertainment the cruise provided. It was oddly comforting to know there was always someone there if needed, but that my space was being respected. At least, until Friday evening.

There was a knock on my door, and I answered it to find one of the crew members with a delivery. The scent of glamour clung to her clothes faintly, so I knew she wouldn't remember coming here or seeing me at all. Still, I thanked her and sent her on her way.

I laid the box on my bed and stared at it for several minutes. Glossy black. Red bow.

With clenched teeth I opened it, lifting out a blue silk dress. I'd never seen anything like it. The pleating was next to identical to the ripples on the river some mornings, but the soft blue resembled the sea more than murky freshwater. It looked like my two worlds colliding and made my heart race.

Against my better judgement I tried it on. The halter neckline was secured by two silver pearls at the nape of my neck. Real ones— I could tell by the feel of them. It wasn't scandalous by any means, but the way it clung to my curves was definitely purposeful.

In the bottom of the box sat a small envelope, and a pair of glittering stilettos that I didn't even want to entertain the cost of. My eyes scanned the scrawling handwriting, unsurprised by who it was from.

I realized I'd asked to take you dancing without even knowing if you were prepared for it. I hope it's not too forward, if you have something else you'd rather wear please feel free to. And yes, Cillian helped me choose because I'm helpless at this kind of thing.

Aleki

My stomach flipped, fingers gripping the small piece of paper ever so slightly tighter.

I'd wanted to go. And he knew it without me even saying anything.

The next knock on my door made me jump, my adrenaline already rushing. And when I opened it Aleki's warm smile greeted me.

"Well, I see that it fits."

22

Renita

"You mean to convince me that you can hike a mountain in the dead of night, but heels are a challenge for you?" Aleki's tease was timed perfectly with another stumble, the toe of my shoe catching on the lip of my doorway. He was there of course, catching me against his side again with ease.

"Shockingly, heels were never a necessity in my life," I grumbled, blushing slightly in embarrassment. I gripped his forearm tightly, wary of how slippery the tiled floor suddenly seemed. He only chuckled, not taunting me further as he led me down the hall.

I had no good reason to be doing what I was doing. I had a million reasons to not to of course, which just made my already wild heartbeat tick even harder.

The way I was wrestling it right now was simply just to enjoy one night. Having the Mer on the mountain was one of the most stressful experiences of my life. And since boarding the yacht I had been on edge every waking moment. I might not be able to allow myself to dive in headfirst, but for a night, I needed to relax. Stop fighting for my life and take a breath before being thrust before the court.

And despite my best efforts, I liked them. Aleki was all charm, and steady. Only a fool wouldn't realize he was a reliable and honest man. And Cillian, the idiot, he'd already made it clear his world would revolve around me if I'd let it. Only more literally than he could imagine.

"There she is!" Nyx, visibly tipsy, was braced halfway between the wall and Leonardo. The sight was shocking enough to silence the brewing typhoon in my head instantly. I felt Aleki tense with a buried laugh, and my own lips wanting to quirk into a smile.

"Oh boy—"

"Now this is nice, so nice. Doesn't she look nice?" Nyx smacked his hand down on Leonardo's shoulder four times while he rambled, making the man grimace outright.

"Sure, she looks nice. Now will you shut up and walk?"

"He doesn't get out much." Aleki's voice was hushed, breath grazing my ear. "And after preoccupying himself with knowing where you were every waking minute these past few weeks, I may had slid him a few drinks harder than I led him to believe so he would finally relax a tad."

"A tad?" I asked, fighting to not smack Aleki or burst into laughter. "He's going to kill you." The man in question had now been herded onto a bench a few paces down the hall, his head flopped into Sylus' lap while Maximus and Leonardo brainstormed on how to handle this rare event.

"I'll be sure to apologize later," Aleki murmurs, shifting his grip to my lower back to guide me towards a set of double doors. "For now, I'd like to make good on my promise if you'll allow it, little predator."

The faint drum of music through the doors did not prepare me for how loud it actually was inside. And the number of bodies pressing and swaying together raged like the river after weeks of storms. Only Aleki's hand on my back, and his other one seamlessly sliding into one of mine, kept me from feeling disoriented.

"Is it bold to assume you've never been to a place like this before?" Aleki had to shout over the beat, something techno and bass colliding in a way that made my ribcage feel like a beating drum itself. I only shook my head, and he laughed, leading me to the far end of a bar along the side of the room. The hand on my back dropped to my ass without warning, and he effortlessly lifted me onto a free bar stool before I could even register it. He caught my eye as he leaned into the tight space beside me, smirking. "Oh please. I figured after having my mouth on you, my hand would be nothing."

"Shut up," I grumbled, but my attention was immediately pulled back to the dance floor. Other than the few college parties I'd indulged in over the years, I had never been to a place anywhere close to this. Inhibition was out the window with almost everyone, the effect of music and drink letting reservation take a back seat. Briefly, I thought it felt like my magic: unruly, untamed, and utterly, perfectly, natural. If not a bit dangerous.

"Would you like a drink?" He asks, and I force my eyes back to him, assessing him as he's done me on more than one occasion. Black dress pants, shining shoes, and pressed white shirt. The sleeves were rolled up his forearms, and all his waves of hair were tied up in a simple knot.

"I'm hoping you don't think I'll wind up like our friend out there?" I feign suspicion and hook my thumb back in the direction of the door for good measure. Aleki's grin deepens, unfettered.

"Do you truly think I would dare?" His grin tilts into a smirk as I purse my lips, squirming.

"No," I relent, grumbling to myself as he laughs, waving over the bartender. I stick to something light, house gin and tonic on the rocks, sipping it lightly as I take in the room again.

"So." I tap my nails on the bar, side eyeing him. "You really did want to take me dancing, huh?"

"There's a million things I would like to do and share with you." The immediate honesty was shocking, making me pay attention to him fully but he just offered a soft shrug. "I figured my best bet was to instigate something small. So that you might take me seriously beyond..." He trailed off, letting me fill in the gaps on my own. I nodded once, a piece of me needing him to know I understood.

"Then shouldn't you be asking me to dance?" I asked quietly, but despite the noise around us I knew he heard. He pushed off the bar, wordlessly extending a hand to me and I took it.

Suddenly I was self-conscious, worried about tripping in my shoes, not moving to the beat right and making a fool of myself. Right before my pride could intervene and make me stop, he tugged me closer, pulling us flat together in the center of the fray.

Based on the grin on his face I'm sure I looked either embarrassed or panicky, but instead of teasing me he just shifted my hands to his neck. One of his legs parted mine, his body easing mine back before his hands pulled me forward again, helping me find rhythm in the chaos around us.

"There you go," he murmured against my hair as I felt myself relaxing, focusing on the music rather than the amount of people. His presence was both electrifying, and a reassurance.

I began to sway on my own, eyes drifting shut, head drifting back. I could feel the power in my veins, pulsing in rhythm to the music which was beating its way through my chest.

Aleki was slow with me this time, his hunger from the mountain replaced by curiosity. He let his touch linger on the places where it made my fingers clench, my breath cut short. Just when it felt like the tension between us was approaching a precipice, he spun me, his arm hooking lazily around my waist to keep me pinned to him.

I let out an involuntary groan. He was hard. And before I could even take a breath there was another grip on my chin, one that I knew intimately.

I froze as Cillian's gaze drifted over me. At my skirt which had ridden up slightly, the way my chest heaved for breath, the blush I felt heating my skin. His expression was damn near unreadable, making my heart race even faster. He lifted his gaze over my shoulder, eyes flashing briefly, and Aleki's grip on my hips instantly tightened.

"O-okay," I stuttered, finally finding my voice. "Look I'm not expecting anything, and obviously the two of you still need to discuss—"

Cillian's mouth on mine silenced me, then devoured the moan that slipped loose when Aleki kissed my pulse.

"Perfect," he groaned, both his hands coming to cup my face while Aleki continued to pepper my skin with kisses and bites. I felt like I was freefalling between them, my hands sliding up Cillian's chest, claws digging in, earning me a moan of my own.

I should stop it here, now. Put this madness and restlessness between us to bed, convince them one way or another to give up their pursuit. But before I could even begin to pull back, I felt a slight tremor rock through the ship.

One that didn't come from the sound equipment across the room, nor a wave. Aleki felt me tense first, his mouth leaving me instantly.

"Renita?" Concern, and blissful unawareness. Cillian equally was focused only on me, but I was shaking my head, blood rushing for a whole other reason now.

"They're here," I said, pushing Cillian forward, dragging Aleki behind me.

"Renita what are you—" suddenly the lights cut, plunging us into black.

Sirens. More than at home. More than I think anyone expected. My heels were forgotten as I ran for the stairs, feeling their song making the air vibrate, the ship shake. Fear had me running cold, clamping my own voice deep in my throat. They would not go quietly. And there were too many people here to waste time trying to convince them to.

I took the stairs two at a time, doing my best not to crash into the tourists racing down. Cries filled the air, people afraid, others shouting orders, trying to regain some semblance of control over a threat they couldn't begin to imagine.

Thankfully due to the hour, the deck was cleared before I even reached it. The night air flooding my lungs was heavy with glamour. And the metallic tang of blood.

The first one I saw was hunched over a man, his shirt torn from his body in the woman's haste to bury her teeth in his neck. He was still conscious, reaching blindly for anything which could help him.

"What are you doing?" I asked, wholly aware my voice was far more melodic than it should be, enough to catch her attention. She released him slowly, sitting up to look me over.

"Starving, sister." I couldn't look at her, could only stare in horror as I watched the man's life force spilling out on the deck beneath him.

"Stop," I breathed, my whole body locked, a live wire about to snap. Her chuckle was even more lyrical than mine. I was coated in a wave of blissful honey and temptation, a burst of floral like a perfect spring day, and then the warm scent of sugared coffee and syrup.

"And there's your fancy," she purred.

I finally looked at her as she stood fully. Pale skin, tinged with blue scales which flashed in the dull emergency lights covering the deck. Fangs. Black pits for eyes. So much like a woman, and so much like a monster.

"You crave a sense of peace, don't you child? A taste of home, wherever that is. Warm, and reassuring." My claws made my own hands bleed as I clenched my fists, her humor finally banking to wariness. "Are you a wanderer?"

Her question didn't even register. My eyes had travelled beyond her to the dozens of women on board, all bloodstained lips, birdsong, and grace. They moved through the air as I imagined they would under the sea: flowing, elegant, seemingly slow motion. Lethal.

I growled sharply, smacking her extended hand away with a force which had her jumping back with a hiss.

"Leave," I ordered, reveling in the way she shuddered. That's right, I was a Queen, and she was just a—

The group of us bristled in synch, but I turned too late. My scream caught in my throat as Sylus dove from above, Maximus right behind him. The two of them were focused on me, on cutting her off from being able to reach me. They didn't see the Sirens in the back, with pulsing blades of water poised and ready.

The shots were silent, striking before the Mer had even hit the deck. And when their bodies fell, the noose I'd had on my magic my whole life snapped.

The force of my power flooding the deck shattered the windows, and rocked the ship on its hull. Each of the Sirens had flown back, a few slamming into the rails which sent a thrill down my spine. A bloodthirsty, rageful, heartbroken thrill. I knew my skin was glowing now, and I let the heady euphony of my glamour soak each word.

"Get in the water."

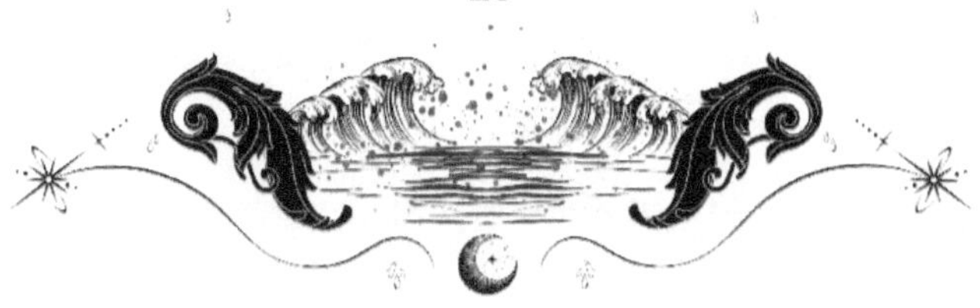

Cillian

Renita had transformed into a creature of scales, and wrath. Even the water clinging to her like liquid fire couldn't hide it. My world was zoned in on her, no matter how much horror was running through my veins. I was hers to command: we all were.

My hand was still poised over my tattoos, my trident ready to be called. Alek had his full weight down against Maximus, both our shirts being used to pressure the wound on his chest, trying to halt the bleeding. Sylus was already gone, his throat severed.

"Get in the water."

The symphonic order flowed around us. I could *taste* it in the air, but it didn't land on me, nor any of my men. The Siren's, however, launched themselves back into the sea like she had thrown them herself. And Renita followed.

Only when her crystalline laughter vanished from the deck could we once again move. Leonardo had Nyx pinned to the wall, his shoulder bleeding from one of the icy strikes which he'd managed to dodge while getting his Warrior out of the way. Nyx was thrashing, screaming, his desperation to follow and keep her safe even now warring with my own.

Mateo and Juan had already flung themselves overboard, and I felt my feet moving before I realized what I was doing.

"Cillian no!" Alek's scream was too late, the world flashing violet around me as I summoned my trident and dove overboard. These monsters had come for me, and instead two of my closest companions were lying dead and dying. I would not be another King who just sat there and allowed it to happen.

The sea was frothing as I submerged, pulsing teal, gold, green— wild magic making it begin to boil. And the screams surrounding me? Dizzying. Delicious. My arms felt numb, but I still cast the incantation, making the ocean itself siphon off me to send wave after wave of power, driving them back.

Juan and Mateo worked in tandem, one circling the other in synch, staying at my back as I advanced into the absolute battle this had become. I could taste blood in the water, felt a bolt of panic that it could be hers. But then lightning stuck the surface just like at the water festival, just like on the mountain when that creature attacked us, and I knew instinctively that she was in one piece.

Screams turned shrill as I surfaced, eyes finding her immediately. She was untouched and walking on the surface of the ocean like one of the

Gods herself. Water rolled over her like a second skin, the brilliant shine of her scales covering every inch of her, each step making her glitter but that wasn't what caught my focus.

Strung along her arms, was sparking cords of electricity, feeding off the roiling storm clouds building above us. Lighting struck another wave, turning the whole thing to glass, which she seamlessly shattered with a volley of ice-tipped arrows. And her voice... breathtaking. Drawing in the next Siren slowly, their eyes glazed over while she incinerated them.

"Your majesty." The mocking feline purr to my left redirected me and I whirled just in time. Juan cried out, but the tip of my trident sank deep into the gut of the Siren who dove for me. She screamed, the sound making me shudder, and launched herself at me with all she had left. I cried out as a whip of water crashed into my ribs, the pain making me see stars.

There was a low hum that seemed to come from the belly of the ocean itself, making time slow, and then the singing of bullets. They rocked the Sirens body, the force of the blow throwing her fully off my trident and beneath the waves.

Through blurred vision my eyes found Renita's again. Her hand was still outstretched in my direction, glittering with remnants of the attack which just saved my life.

There were no more Siren songs staining the air, no more shrill whistles and clicks, and the sudden quiet made me nauseous immediately.

Juan surfaced with my trident; I hadn't even
realized I lost my grip on it. And Mateo's insistent
grip on my side had me cursing, trying to apply
pressure to whatever the hell had been done to me
as the waves lapped at us. And I was still staring
at her, standing on the surface of the sea, eyes
clenched shut looking like she was in pure agony
as she collapsed her magic back in on itself.

"Cillian!" Alek was in the water now too,
his face suddenly blocking my sight of her.
Whatever he was shouting I couldn't hear.
Everything was dizzy, and hot, way too hot for the
North Atlantic.

"Cillian." Melodic, but not entrapping. I
could feel the scrape of sharp teeth, but instead of
pain, heat flooded me as I finally succumbed to
the embrace of the waves.

Cillian

I heard the gulls first. Then the gentle lap of waves.

"Easy." Alek's scent flooded my nose as I lurched upright, straight into his arms which began easing me back. "She did something which countered the poison, but you're still not in great shape."

"Where is she?" I croaked out, my throat feeling burnt like sand during a drought. Poison? The hell was he talking about?

"She's safe." The way he said it instantly made me tense. And he was avoiding my gaze now too.

"Alek, she saved us," I started but his fist slammed the arm of his chair, silencing me. It wasn't often he let his anger get the best of him, so I wasn't about to argue with it. Not when I was finally beginning to get feeling back in my spent body, and most of it felt like my ribs had been punctured.

"Cillian please stay down," he said, voice as raw as I felt but I still pushed his hands off me anyway. I dragged myself to my feet, gaping at my reflection in the mirror.

My entire right side was covered with twisting purple burns, blistering at the edges where they met my tattoos. I felt nausea rising in the back of my throat so averted my gaze, motioning for the mirror to be taken away too.

"That last bitch somehow manipulated the water to sting you like a Man-O-War," he explained, settling beside me and urging my good side to lean against him. "Renita bit you after you were unconscious, drank the poison out of your blood."

"Is she insane?" I asked, hearing my voice shake as a shiver rocked my body. "That could have killed her."

"She had a fever, but it broke yesterday," he grumbled, and I elbowed him, sick of the shitty attitude.

"We would all be dead if not for her."

"Yea, well. Two of us are anyway." The pain rocketing through my chest made me entirely forget about the wound on my side. Alek already had the trash can in front of me as the vomit came up, the memory of our friend's blood staining the deck making me want to scream.

"We gave their spirits a proper release before returning their bodies to the water," Alek murmured, trying to sound strong but I heard the crack in his voice too. Something that he noted as well, his anger instantly flaring to drown out the pain.

"I was raised to protect you above all else," he snapped, abandoning my side to pace through the room. "That is my role, my duty, and my honor. And yet I couldn't sense the danger you had been in this entire trip because I was blindly infatuated with her." While he ranted, I eased back down, silently withdrawing my trident from my untouched tattoo and letting its familiar weight anchor me.

"You were not blindly infatuated with her. I've seen you like that, and it's gross." I'd hoped that the joke would have eased some of the tension in the air, but it only served to make it worse.

"She'd glamoured me so excessively," he snarled, fist pounding on the dresser. "Most likely so that she could get close to you!"

Though I wanted to argue it vehemently, I could not. Too many things made sense now, knowing what she truly was. Her ability to talk herself out of any situation, the thick taste of her magic coating the world whenever it surfaced, and the uncontrollable way she stole my breath with anything she did. I too had felt the pull Alek described. At first, I thought it was witchcraft, something heavy and foreign that I just wasn't used to. But then after her tail had been revealed, I had imagined, nearly prayed, that the Gods sent her for me. And... perhaps they had.

"So then why am I not dead?" Silence followed my question, and in it I pushed to my feet, resting my weight on my trident.

"You've said it yourself a million times," I said softly, my brain already working faster than my mouth could keep up. "Sirens, the monsters they are, are simple creatures. They do not think beyond attacking. They do not hesitate once they have an opening. And they most definitely do not practice restraint. So surely, she would have satiated her thirst with me by now, or at the very least had killed one of you herself, rather than saving us repetitively."

I'd crossed to him while I spoke, raising my grip to cup his cheek now, and pressed a kiss to his mouth. I wasn't sure if I was trying to calm him or myself at this point. Nothing made sense anymore.

"She's even siphoned off of me, Alek. Before whatever connection between us had the time to develop. And she did me no harm."

I had been shocked by the draw of power she'd pulled from me the night of the water festival, but had been so focused on the immediate threat that I hadn't lingered on it. I dropped my forehead to his chest, heaving a frustrated sigh.

"I'm not trying to convince you of anything other than she's not some monster hidden in our midst. This is something else. Something we've never dealt with before."

"A royal Siren," he groaned painfully, following my thoughts and I nodded. I felt his chin drop to my shoulder, hand gripping my good hip painfully, but I said nothing. "I'm so fucking angry and confused."

"I know," I murmured, smoothing his hair. "But screaming at her won't do any good. There are obvious reasons why she chose not to tell us, but the rest of it... I want to know why."

The gears in my brain had shifted. She and I had spoken about the Siren problem before, and I thought she was bold for suggesting they weren't all evil. I had harbored the same beliefs, but they were not appropriate opinions at court. Especially not without proof. And now, as much as I hated it, I had somehow captured a Siren to my side who defended me against her own kin. That was a fact that no one in court would have anything prepared to attack or overturn.

"Where is she?" I asked again, pulling back to look him in the eye. He hesitated, his desire to protect me warring with our unstable reality.

"She's in her room. The twins haven't left her side." I breathed a small sigh of relief, but Alek held me fast when I'd moved to go. "You're not going to like the state that she's in, but know she insisted."

I felt my stomach flip, a chill running through me. If she wasn't being treated outright like a prisoner, then that could only mean—

Alek forced me to slow down, keeping me glued to his side as a strangled sound tore through me at the sight of her. The warmth of her skin had been nearly drained, making her look sickly. Her eyes shifting to me barely held any of her fire, only holding my gaze for a minute before going back out the window.

"She won't allow us to remove it," Juan said softly, sensing my rising anger before even I could.

Embedded in her neck was a collar of enchanted coral. The rough tips tore at her skin where tiny hooks sank in, the veins in her neck bulging and black. I didn't even know we had been carrying one of those with us, my accusatory gaze landing on Leonardo who was standing over her, his arms crossed.

"Remove it at once," I growled, feeling my power flair through me despite my weakened state.

"And get scratched and bit at again?" Leonardo scoffed, avoiding my gaze. "No thanks."

I finally noticed Nyx in the corner of the room, even more drawn into himself than normal. Feeling my eyes, he turned his head, and I gaped. Three angry claw marks had been torn across his cheek, and I whipped my gaze back to her.

"Renita," I said, hearing my own voice break. "Why are you doing this?"

"Why are you arguing it?" She responded. Voice like silk but not making my head hazy as it

often did before I realized. She shifted, pain
visible on her face, but remained poised. "You're
about to walk a Siren into your precious court.
Without it, I'll be thrown into a cell, or just killed
on the spot because they won't trust that I won't
attack." I gripped my trident harder, my rage
growing, knowing she was right.

"I'll order them down," my voice shook
hard enough to rattle the furniture. "No one will
touch you."

Alek's hand was on my shoulder, unafraid
of the violet drips of power falling from my skin
that I couldn't seem to control. She finally turned
to me again, and her smile was devastating.

"And you'll be branded a traitor."

I exploded. I wasn't sure if it was rage or
desperation, but it was out of my control. The
windows shattered, the ship bucking beneath us
on a rogue wave. The mirror skittered across the
floor in a million pieces, glittering in a
constellation which mimicked the glow of her tail,
and a sob wrenched from me.

She hadn't moved, didn't even glance at
me. It was like she didn't care what she was
putting me, putting all of us through. My hand
gripped her hair, yanking her head back, forcing
her to look at me whether she wanted to or not.

"Why did you even come with us?" The
others were surrounding us in an instant, their
trust in her wavering as I embedded the trident

into the wall beside her head, and still, she didn't flinch. "I don't understand."

Finally, some type of emotion from her, the dead look in her eye giving way to something dark and shattered.

"I didn't know how to refuse and... I stayed because you don't deserve to die."

Unconsciously, my hand dropped to her neck, to the coral muting her power and she hissed.

"Don't!" Claws dug into my wrist, her gaze outright pleading. "You cannot deny what you saw—"

"I saw you save us!" Why could she not understand that? Was our world that corrupt? Did she really view herself as a demon even after everything she had done to prove otherwise?

She did, I knew she did. The moment the exclamation left my mouth, she reverted. Eyes shuttered, hands closing over her ears, like a child being tormented by nightmares and believing them to be reality. I did not know how to save her from herself, but I'd be damned if I wouldn't try to save her from my world.

"Leave her," I murmured, vying to keep my voice even now, calm, collected. An emotional meltdown on my part would do nothing to drag her from the depths from which she was intent to drown herself. I glanced at each of my men in turn, daring them to oppose me. "See that she eats, and rests. We'll handle this properly when we arrive at Illes Balears. She is not to be harmed or humiliated. Am I understood?"

A series of nods, a few clenched jaws, but I was satisfied enough. Mateo alone remained in the room, the others following me back to my suite. I ignored Alek's request to return to bed, pacing fervently for many minutes.

"Nyx," I murmured, pausing. "Have your cuts been treated?"

"Yes, my King," he responded, low, aching.

"How did you get them?" I pressed, needing to know there was no mistake in my assumptions. Needing every ounce of physical proof on my side for what I intended to do.

"I tried removing the coral in her sleep." Nyx sounded pained through the admission. "You are my King. I will follow your orders. But she is my Queen... I cannot bear to see her in pain, even if it is by her choice."

"It was still idiotic," Leonardo grumbled, but his worry for his Warrior was painfully evident.

"Leonardo. The two of you seem to have the most strained relationship." I shifted, not letting them distract themselves. "Did you ever sense a threat from her when you pushed her?"

"Other than her hunting on the mountain, no," he admitted begrudgingly. "If anything, I've read her as more desperate than threatening."

"Juan?" I pivoted, locking eyes with the Warrior, and he snorted softly. "Mi rey, she's done nothing an enemy would do. You know this."

"Aleki?" He stiffened but I didn't back down, going straight for the root. "The two of you were alone, and quite intimate. Surely, there would have been something taken, or a threat made?" The look on his face reflected my own experience with her. She was a force, yes, but that had never been used against us even in our most vulnerable moments.

"We will bring her with us as a formal prisoner," I say, each of them snapping to look at me in shock. I just smirked. "Relax. She's a Mer cursed to live without a tail, isn't that right, Nyx?"

A small smile quirked the corner of his mouth, a bit of life returning to his eyes. "Yes, my King." I grinned, finally settling back down on the bed.

"Good. Though that option has escaped us, here's what we're going to do."

25

Renita

Over the past few days, Cillian nor Aleki visited me again, and I didn't blame them. Cillian was injured; he shouldn't have risked coming before me to begin with. I'd barely been able to concentrate on what he said. The coral, though stifling my magic, wasn't muting it completely. The scent of blood still clung to each of his pores, his power exposed in his weak state, making my fangs ach in my mouth. And Aleki, well, his strength and protection had returned wholly to Cillian's side. I needed to stop pretending like I'd deserved any of it to begin with.

Despite the injury I caused, Nyx visited every day. I was grateful for his presence in the silence. We did not have to speak for me to sense the war within him, torn between remaining loyal to his world, or a singular woman in his life. Leonardo though was more outwardly hateful than I'd ever seen. Again, something deserved for my actions and secrets.

The twins hadn't changed a thing about the function of relationship, other than somehow being more stoic than before. I was watched in shifts, the air less like I was being looked after, and more like I was finally the prisoner that I should have been the whole time.

I don't know how I kidded myself into believing I could avoid this. From the moment they showed up at Cora's diner, I should have realized this would have been my fate. I was a Siren. I could never be a part of their world, even though for a moment, I had wanted to be.

And sleep plagued me. The coral exhausted me more than I was prepared for, but it was a precaution I couldn't risk denying. My magic was rampant. I could feel the wild urges like never before, threatening to take over in whole. I thought I had learned how to control it, but turns out, it was only suppressed this whole time.

I tossed and turned through nightmares of stormy seas, of my mother's screams being swallowed by crashing waves and rock. Violet lightning singeing my skin, and beasts with gaping jaws draining me dry while I watched.

Upon waking from one of these nightmares, I was surprised to find Aleki standing by the window. A quick glance at the room proved we were alone.

"Cillian requested the others to prepare. We'll be slipping off this ship just before daybreak." His voice was clipped, body tense as he remained faced away from me.

"…We've arrived at the Mer Court, then?" I asked slowly, my tongue feeling as if it were rubbed raw with sandpaper from disuse.

"We entered the Balearic Sea a few hours ago." His gaze finally slides to mine, and rather than the anger I expected, it's full of raw vulnerability. "Was any of it real?" He asks, eyes searching mine. "Anything I felt? That Cillian felt? Or was it all a glamour?"

Despite the pain radiating through my body, and the constant awareness of my insatiable hunger, I could feel the heat staining my cheeks, blushing like a fool.

"I only glamoured you when I needed to protect you," I whispered, shaking slightly even though I was covered by blankets. "The Wendigo attack, the… Sirens. And to stay away. I never intended to get close to any of you. This was the opposite of what I wanted."

"What did you want?" He snapped, suddenly atop me, straddling my legs and pinning me down. His fingers dug into my chin hard enough to bruise, his eyes wild as he glared down at me. "Why did you even leave your Coven? Did you know nothing of the consequences you might face in our world?"

"Your world," I whispered, and he jolted as if I slapped him.

"I'm a Siren." My voice shook as I said it, and I realized it might be the first time I ever had. "I was barred from your world upon birth. Deemed too dangerous, too much of a hazard. Uncontrollable." I hardened my voice as much as I could, unwilling to allow what remaining pieces of me there were to break. "You saw what I can do. The destruction. The chaos."

"I saw you turn on your own people in favor of your enemy," he growled, just as unwilling to relent as I was. A laugh bubbled out of me, unable to help myself.

"We know there's only one ending to this, Aleki."

"There's only one ending if you continue to stubbornly not explain yourself." Despite his harsh tone, his eyes were impossibly soft. "Why did you stay with us Renita? Why didn't you flee the other night after what you'd done?"

My blood was rushing in my ears, the coral on my throat burning in response to the sweep of magic that shook the room around us. Aleki didn't budge as the wave of it hit him, though he looked stunned that I could manage so much in my state. To me, it felt very little. I was unable to focus, to breathe, until he lifted me by the shoulders, slamming me back down to the bed.

"God damn it Renita, what do you want!?"

"I don't know!" A sob tore from my throat but he didn't let me go. He caught my wrists in one of his hands when I began scratching at him and pinned them above my head, and I screamed outright in my frustration.

I wanted to go home. To not be on this stupid deathtrap of a trip to begin with. My panic after the water festival, and my naivety of this world, is what dragged me here.

But it is not what kept me. I had never felt alone in the Coven. I knew I was loved but we were always off balance. I had to be subdued to not cause fear, and those in my presence were often more austere than they were naturally for me to feel as if I fit in place.

Being with the Mer had been easy. Terrifyingly so. It had less to do with physical chemistry which, honestly, I'd prefer. It would be easier to explain or make an excuse of. This emotional depth between me and each of them was threatening to drown me before I could fully comprehend it.

Their presence provided a sense of inarguable solace, and the pieces of me which often wanted to shatter lost the urge. And when my tendencies slipped out, there had been no ruffle, no panic. It had even been encouraged in the mountains. Even now, I was being handled like a jewel despite the danger I was to them. Terror did not begin to describe how I felt when faced with losing them, and the freedom and acceptance this small bubble of time provided.

Aleki had not let up his grip in the slightest, his eyes searching mine as I cried beneath him. Why wasn't he running? Why wasn't I dead? I should be dead, I should be—

"Little predator…" He gently dragged me upright, and I was too weak to fight against him as he leaned back, shifting me to lay on top of him. The heat from his body flooded me, his steady heartrate against my ear dousing the panic from my system until the breaths I was sucking in slowed and matched the deep ones he took. His fingers were shifting through my hair, grazing down my spine, and for the first time in days when sleep came for me, the nightmares did not.

Renita

Dawn came quickly, the first lilac hues coasting atop the ocean's waveless surface before I had the energy to move.

"Renita." Aleki hadn't left me, and that somehow made everything simultaneously worse and better. He gazed down at me gently, but I could see the restraint there. Him mentally preparing for what was to come.

The water felt like a prison now. All the relief and wanting and release it had given me just a few short days ago utterly drained to something hollow and dark. We weren't far from the coast. Fishing boats were passing by the cruise ship, dodging like how I'd imagine krill would a whale. I didn't get to look at anything more than that before they took me down.

It was impossible to not transform. The poison in the coral lessened my grip of control over everything. As we dove, I was bound by a rippling tie of gold, connected to both Nyx and Aleki. In case I attempted to bolt, I assumed. Cillian though, had done something which forced a laugh from me, the sound grating and wrong.

"I knew it," I breathed out, fascinated as his diamond tail shifted to a deep blue. "At the very least, after this, let my aunt know that her hypothesis was right." He hadn't replied, didn't so much as look at me, but I was content.

There was no visible barrier between the Mer Court and the surface world, but the drag of magic against my skin was tangible, like the slow pull of molasses. Colors became both brighter, and more translucent. Fish shifted, many appearing bizarrely similar to lesser fae, tangling in my hair or whizzing past.

The reef we were heading towards was nondescript, but the immediate flash of scales had me bristling. We were surrounded by Mer in a half a second, armored, with weapons ranging from serrated coral to polished swords.

"Majesty?" The voice came from behind us, and a massive Mer which I could only assume reflected some type of ancient shark was swimming towards us. Though he addressed Cillian, his gaze was on me. Hard, and unforgiving. "This creature—"

"Yes." Cillian interrupted, and a smile I'd never seen on his face before made me want to wither. Oppressive. Haughty. And outwardly entertained. "I've managed to catch one of the beasts."

My heart shattered, but I refused to move. Summoning my rage instead of tears, locking myself down to not feel a damn thing because if I did...

"Do we know what she is?"

"A Manipulative, mainly." Aleki this time, equally as cruel as Cillian. "Both in nature, and behavior." The three of them shared a laugh at my expense. I wanted to argue, to defend myself somehow. At the very least, the shade of my scales should mean something in their strict world, yes?

Desperately I glanced down and was unable to help the sharp sound of shock and mortification which tore from my throat. The smattering of black on my hips had stained me wholly, my tail shifting to the darkest night. I couldn't have done this. I couldn't have been so desperate to hide that I'd unconsciously condemned myself further.

Nyx's hand between my shoulders continued to propel me forward before Aleki could drag me. I was so stunned I couldn't focus. I knew I should be paying attention to every detail, layout at the very least as we sunk deeper into the reef, weaving through a series of illuminated corridors below. If there was any possibility of getting out of here, I would need to retrace our path.

Or just blow the whole reef apart.

Aleki swung to look at me, wide eyed as I snarled, unable to help myself. I had let them collar me. Been compliant. Saved their fucking backstabbing lives! Nyx yanked the back of my neck sharply, the coral biting deeper and making me see white until I screamed.

"Such dramatics," he cooed, making me continue to spiral further. "Be silent and wait."

The throbbing in my neck had spread to my whole body by the time we emerged in a room so bright I shuddered. The whole thing had to be carved from a gigantic pearl, as impossible as that was to comprehend. The milky iridescence of the walls couldn't be anything else. I was yanked to a halt, the ties on my hands pulling taught, forcing me to hang suspended with my arms drawn wide.

Humiliation coursed through me as the eyes of the court surveyed me. There weren't many, maybe a dozen or so nobles, their tails shining crimson, ruby, and blood orange. The only others were the guards who escorted us inside. Roughly forty Mer, whose sole purpose here was subduing me should I lash out.

"She's less impressive than I thought one of them would be."

A Mer at the edge of the crowd, with eyes a shade of plum so terrifyingly similar to the violet I was used to, spoke while edging forward. His tail shone a brilliant gold, and I knew in an instant that this was the Mer King. As Cillian had shown, a royal could change the color of their tail. And if his previous attitude about the King reflected anything, he was chauvinistic enough to make himself gold like he was worth more than anything in the room.

A silent snarl curled my lips again, flashing my fangs briefly and I gained the desired result. The fucker stayed back.

"Her actions wouldn't fail to impress you, father." I whipped my gaze to Cillian, unable to help myself. He didn't look at me. "She didn't even have to shift to kill twelve of her own." At that, the Mer King laughed heartily.

"Oh? Have they finally resorted to destroying themselves?" He swam away, resting on an opaque clam shell with an identical golden cushion as his scales. "That will make our future far easier to secure."

"On the contrary..." This time, Cillian's twisted smile was on his father. "She's been in our company for the better part of two months. Has been functioning as more of a guard dog, rather than a vigilante."

The King looked between me and his son, like he was missing the piece of some puzzle.

"Are you expecting me to believe—"

"She killed another Siren after it attacked me." Cillian interrupts unabashedly, and gestures to the angry purple wound still decorating his right side. "Along with its twenty or so companions, with frankly, little help from us. She also killed some type of cryptid which attacked us while we travelled through the mountains she calls home. And she's siphoned off me directly without causing any immediate harm."

"Are you blasted mad!" The Kings voice shook the room, silencing the murmuring and giggles from our audience. His eyes flashed with predatory intent, moving like a whip through the water to grab Cillian by the face. I lunged at him, fangs poised to tear his throat out, but Nyx yanked me back again. I was hissing and thrashing in his grip, like I was truly as wild as they believed.

Slowly, the King studied my face. I have no idea what he found there, but it had him looking back at his son like he was the most pathetic creature he'd ever laid eyes on.

"...Has this creature truly seduced you?" Aleki bristled by my side, a growl resonating deep in his throat which the King ignored. "Really Cillian, I would have thought better of you."

Finally, *finally*, Cillian's gaze met mine. The storms in his eyes swelling as wildly as the one brewing in my chest. I felt the tension from my bonds loosen as Aleki curled in front of me, growling louder. Every inch of him was poised in erratic defiance as he placed himself directly between the King and I. Nyx had pressed to my spine, Leonardo by his side, and the twins were stationed on either side of me.

It happened so fast I almost missed it. Almost. That wink of violet power surfacing in Cillian's eyes. And the way that deep ocean belly blue faded from him completely, leaving him gleaming. Just as I knew my blackened scales had shifted back to silver, sending the room into an uproar.

A few of the nobles instantly fled, just as some of the guards surrounding us lowered their weapons uncertainly. The King had loosened his hold on Cillian enough for him to slip away, drifting closer to our group.

"You always said it was the crowns duty to maintain the balance of power. Was always your favorite argument when advocating for another hunt or raid that would undoubtedly kill several of our people."

Aleki shifted only for Cillian to reach me, Nyx at my back not moving an inch as I tried to back away.

"Don't!" I hissed, my freed hands coming up to cover my mouth and nose. I was too worked up, the hope of balancing on that precipice obliterated as I fought the slow motion free fall off it.

"Your idea of balance," Cillian growled, continuing to berate his father without a care of the danger he was in. "Is hoarding it. Controlling it. And if you can't do either of those, eradicating it." His fingers drifted along my neck, gentle against the coral buried in my skin. Then ripped it out.

I caught myself on Aleki's shoulder, gasping and coughing, my blood staining the water around us as I took my first full breath in days. Nails sharpened to points, ripples of my power slinking out and away from me, violet clinging to their edges.

"I've seen true balance now," Cillian murmurs, smoothing my hair while I desperately try to collect myself. A hand is slipping into mine, Aleki's rough calluses sliding against me gently.

"Renita is living proof of true balance. Living amongst both humans and supernatural's alike. A formidable sense of control even now when her bloodlust is so evident. And a true balance to the power of water. Perhaps father, the rule does not apply to Sirens because they are truly meant to be the ones who rule. Perhaps, the Mer are limited in our strengths, left to selfishly drain ourselves of magic if we dare to crave more than our limits. And perhaps, you have forgotten our most sacred rule of all."

He curved my face into his neck, and I shattered, fangs finally digging in and taking what I had unconsciously craved for years. Aleki's hands on my hips. Cillian's mouth pressing to the top of my head. And such a glorious taste of relief that I moaned into his skin as I drank.

"If you weren't my son, I would hang you to dry out," the King growled viciously. A wave of enraged, wine tinted power made the room around us groan, a crack appearing in the ceiling above.

A low, sultry warning sound pulsed through the water from my chest as I retracted my fangs. Slowly licking the blood off my lips, I raised my gaze to the King, tilting my head to a predatory, assessing angle. The rage on his face flickered briefly and I groaned. I could taste his fear. I wanted more of it.

"Our most sacred rule," Cillian repeated, sounding deliciously breathless behind me, "is that power is not handed down through familial lines. Your seed did not birth a King: the Gods willed it. Just as they willed Renita here, now."

The water swelled around us in a way it shouldn't be able to in a space this condensed, following the flow of my breath, my energy. And I smiled.

"You're seriously siding with that creature?" The King spat, withdrawing a sword from his spine, where I'm sure a tattoo like his sons lay. Cillian's trident appeared in response, his teeth bared in a wild smile.

The guards around us had begun pressing back in, the Mer at my sides circling, daring them to attack me. Their Queen.

"I'm formally challenging your hold on the throne, father. I suggest you find a willing Empath to work with you against us." My skin crawled with anticipation, finally realizing what was coming next. Cillian's eyes went wholly violet, and my hand slid to his spine.

"Mi tesoro," he purred, our magic mixing at the contact. "Use me."

I didn't have to be told twice. The pearled room around us gave a small shudder, the Kings

only warning before rupturing and the ocean
rushed in.

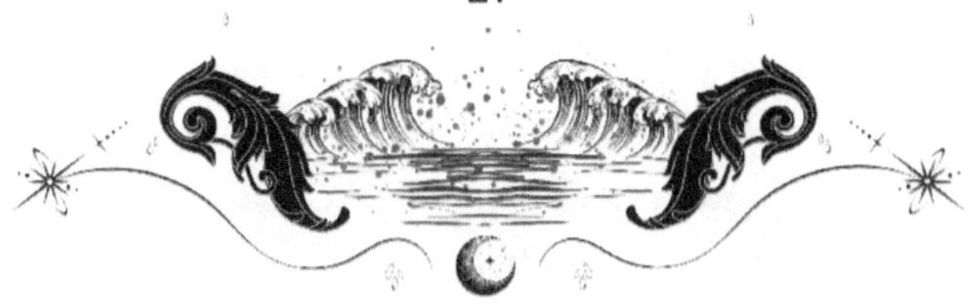

Cillian

Alek's laugher boomed as the fine dust around us settled, getting swept away on the natural tide. I felt her wince behind me, like she had regretted the destruction she caused, but I loved it. It was after all, a gaudy ass throne room.

As expected, my father hid behind his guards. At least the few who were either brave or stupid enough to cling to outdated duties. I'd always thought his power was wasted— a Warrior's strength in a coward's body. I made a note of each of the guards faces as my men distracted and parried. They would be gracelessly discharged, if not arrested.

Dead if they touched her.

"Breathe tesoro," I tried to reassure, but my own voice was breathless as I felt the next draw of power she took from me. I gave it willingly. The sensation made me feel high, my skin running with the energy of a million little electric tap dances, leaving me feeling saturated and light. Again, her skin was covered in liquid fire, pulsing from green, to blue, to violet and back, the flickering citrus edges curling over me from the proximity. I welcomed the burn just as I'd welcomed her teeth in my skin. I was ravenous for all of her, but my hunger could wait.

I wasn't the only one her power touched or fueled. Streams of it bubbled off her, lighting each of my men up, and only then did I understand the magnitude of my own claims. The balance, the power— she was one of all in this moment. A Siphon for who needed, an Empath for another, a Manipulative and a Warrior and *her*.

The guards fled, feeling the draw of power from her that filled the caverns of my own body. I knew she would want to drain them, and I was inclined to allow her in whichever way she wished.

"Satiate that thirst tesoro, hold nothing back." My hand found hers, doing what I could to anchor her in the chaos. She shuddered against my spine, nails digging in once again, but I remained focused on her actions rather than the bite of pleasure her touch caused.

Watching it seemed inconsequential, minute even, but I could tell the moment their power was stripped from their bodies. Their scales lost their gleam, their faces turned haunted, and the plunge of energy in my ribs was so deep I gasped outright.

"Cillian?" Alek's widened eyes were on my body, on the muscle tissue healing, on the bubbling purple blisters on my ribs fading with each breath of power she drew from my father's guards to heal me. And, I realized, from him as well.

"Renita?" I blinked, turning to face her fully. My gaze cut between her and the tendrils of power straining in the water between the pair.

"C-can't stop," she whispered, and I believed her. Her arms were locked out, fingertips stained black. Her eyes were gleaming jade, showing only power, not her. She was somewhere trapped within it. The tears streaming down her face, clinging to her scaled skin, were proof enough.

"One of us must die," she wheezed, like she was locked in a trance. My eyes cut to my father. His face was contorted in pain, and rage. Despite what she was doing to him he still drew his sword, and I felt the cards shift beyond the playing field I was on. This was personal now, in a way I didn't expect.

"You were already supposed to be dealt with, you demoness!" Alek grabbed me and dove out of the way of the blast of boiling water he sent for her.

"Cillian!" She sobbed, and I breathed a sigh of relief, hearing her voice even as embers continued to boil the water surrounding us. "I have to kill him." Her scream was raw. Primal. And absolutely terrified.

Alek didn't stop me this time. This time he was right at my hip, the two of us shooting back to her, to somehow hold her together while the rest of everything collapsed. A snarl left me as I blocked my father's next blow with my trident and whirled on him myself.

The years of laziness had caught up with him. The years of disuse and affluence making it all too easy to snap the blade of his sword off the hilt like a toothpick.

"Yield." It took me a moment to realize the voice was mine, cold and unwavering. A command I rarely dared allow myself to give, but it was high time I stepped into my own power with how she was battling for me.

I pressed the tip of my trident up to the skin of his throat, his slow swallow making it bob. Renita was still crying behind me, Alek snarling once in response, but I tuned them out. Slowly, I took a breath, drawing those tendrils of her glittering power toward me, and began siphoning my father's strength away from him myself. I would not make her shoulder this, not after everything she has given me.

Slowly, the gold bled out of his scales, muting them back to their natural dull tin. Throughout my life at least, he never truly shined to begin with. It was like the Gods themselves had given up on him a long time ago and were waiting for me to get out of my own way. And, hah, apparently, I had taken too long. I was certain this was why they had brought her into my life.

Nyx bound my father's wrists in the same enchanted kelp we had earlier placed on Renita. She cried out again behind me, drawing my attention away from the unworthy King before me. I turned to find Alek digging his pointed teeth into the juncture of her shoulder and neck. He'd clearly done the same to the other side, a mark blooming like a rose against her skin.

"C-can't stop." She was looking at me frantically, and it was only then that I realized she was still drawing power from us.

"Oh, you'll stop little predator," Alek growled, his hand circling her throat. "Even if I need to push you to the point of screaming, you'll stop."

My thumb drew across her bottom lip and her eyes flickered. The burning pits of power briefly shifting back to her emerald, a shade deeper than even the ocean itself. I drew her lower lip between my teeth, pearl and all, sucking hard. And the sound she rewarded me with? Heavenly.

"I know you need more, tesoro," I purred, and she shook. "But not our power. We'll satisfy that hunger of yours another way."

She whipped her hand toward my face, but I just chuckled as I caught her wrist. Threading our fingers I ignored the bite of her claws, and moved my own mouth to her neck, biting down hard. Her pulse was thundering, like something ancient was about to erupt against my tongue.

"Calm," I murmured against her skin. Alek had wound his free hand through her hair,

yanking her head back and baring her to me. I
grazed my teeth against her, relishing in the
effect it had. "Come back to your body, Renita.
You did so well."

The thrashing of her tail had subsided as
my mouth continued south. Alek's tongue played
against the bite marks on her neck, while I
imprinted a fresh one on the curve of her breast,
her breath hitching sharply. But she was
breathing again, and that's all I cared about.

My hands locked on her hips as I snuck a
look up at her, grinning when I met her gaze. A
bolt of relief went through me; her eyes had gone
back to normal. Scales still covered every inch of
her but now glittered like a fine mist on her
cheekbones rather than threatening to overtake
her.

"Better?" I asked. Alek released his grip
on her hair, and she nodded slowly. I lingered for
a moment more, lips pressing gently to her navel
in the way I knew from experience she liked,
before giving up my pursuit. I could see the
exhaustion in her eyes, which made guilt roll
through me for what I was about to do.

"Are you well, my Queen?" I asked. The
question had an instant ripple effect, carried by
the rising tide in the cavernous space. My men
straightened. Alek had dropped his hold on her
and moved to my side. The nobles and guards
curious enough to wander closer in the silence
seemed to hold their breath, knowing exactly

what I implied as Renita stared at me in a mixture of shock and fear.

"No... Cillian don't—"

"Oh, it's much too late for that," I cut her off, my smile widening a fraction before I tucked my chin. Alek followed the motion, then Nyx, Jaun, Mateo. Leonardo paused only to glare at our onlookers, a challenge to defy before he too tucked his head in subservience.

"It is with great pride and relief, that I welcome you home, my Queen," I said, the only one here to raise their head and meet her gaze. "We have been waiting for you."

28

Renita

I felt like I was going to be sick. Ten minutes ago, I was dragged before the Mer court to die. Now, led by Cillian, each and every Mer was bowing... to me. For me? Both options made my head spin till I saw stars.

"Cillian no," I started, but he cut me off. His smile, so easy, so sure. By his side, Aleki snuck a grin at me, but it was Leonardo who cleared his throat.

"You need to verbalize that we may rise, Renita."

"Good Gods get up! Everyone up!" If I could pace I would. My throat was still raw from the coral, my wrists still vibrating from the steady thrum of energy that the binds had enraptured me with. And my head was pounding with what felt like the worst hangover in my life.

The nobles had begun to mutter quietly amongst themselves again, earning a chilling glare from Cillian which quieted them. Most of them.

"This is absurd!"

The ki— former King was now yelling straight in Nyx's face. The Warrior visibly took great pleasure in dragging him backwards through the water a few feet, then whipping him to a stop so quickly his teeth clacked together. He worked his jaw for a moment, groaning uncomfortably, but his glare on me never wavered. "This was supposed to be dealt with years ago."

"Dealt with?" I could have sworn a bolt of icy water cut through the warmth of the Balearic Sea. This time, it was Cillian who was glimmering with power and rage, tendrils of violet latching around his father's throat so hard I could see the veins pulsing in protest. "What do you mean, dealt with?" He demanded, voice so low it was barely more than a growl.

The former King gurgled something, but Cillian didn't let up his hold to let him speak. He was far too gone.

"My King..." one of the nobles had shifted forward, their blood orange tail a blazing contrast in the low light which blanketed the space.

"I did not take the blasted throne!" Cillian snapped, his tone as scathing as his gaze. "You shall address your Queen or be silent." The noble

gave a brief, grotesque look, before fixing his face
and addressing me.

"My Queen... what the former King
speaks of is a... cleansing ritual from about fifteen
years ago."

"Cleansing?" Cillian hissed. For all of
Cillian's ice, my blood had gone colder, all sense of
presence leaving me as a bolt of dreaded
realization went through me.

"Fourteen," I corrected, my voice so quiet I
wasn't sure any of them could hear me. "It was
fourteen years ago."

I could feel the tide curling around me,
back and forth, back and forth. My only source of
heat through the chill was Aleki's hand which
found the base of my spine, holding me steady.
The nobles gaze had settled on me, and I could
practically see the similar wave of realization
dawning on him at my words.

"You were the child there... weren't you."
It wasn't a question, but a hushed bomb going off
between us. Fear rippled off him, but I could not
savor it, I was far too numb. Cillian's shock and
concern interfered with the grip he had on his
father, and the rasped accusation he shot at me
hit its mark.

"The beast before you used her cursed
magic to switch the color of her and her mothers'
tails. So, it was her mother we stripped of scales
and sent to the bottom of the sea."

I wanted the sea to swallow me whole. My shoulders were shaking, as was the sea floor. What little energy I had left remained adamant on holding myself back.

"So, you're admitting you tried to kill a royal?" Was it Cillian's voice, or Aleki's? I knew it wasn't Nyx, he was in front of me now, his usually passive face twisted into something pained.

"To preserve the safety of our world, yes." My face was buried in Nyx's chest now, and Leonardo replaced Aleki at my back as he and the twins went to Cillian's side.

"They're dangerous Cillian! The lot of them! A Siren's magic can't be trusted. We were nearly wiped out because of them!" I could hear them struggling but couldn't move. I would kill someone this time, and I didn't trust myself to be able to control who.

I killed my mother and he knew.

I killed her and—

"Renita."

The old King was gone. The guards, the court and... my Mer remained. The formers gazes were hooded, with either wariness or reverence making their pupils dilate. But my boys... there was so much tenderness and patience there that they would never be able to convince me I deserved. Despite the pain throttling my body, I finally felt something click into place, like a ligament being reset.

Even if I dragged myself out of the sea
again. Even if I climbed back into those
mountains and sank myself back into the hollow
of my river, they would follow.

"Renita." Cillian's voice drifted through
the odd sense of calm within me now, bringing me
back, finding my eyes. He smiled softly, that
damning smile I'd tried but failed to fight.

"I need to ask," he said, gripping my chin
as I started to look away, bracing myself for the
accusation. But it didn't come. His thumb brushed
my cheek, even dared flit over one of the tips of
my exposed fangs as he gently asked, "After the
amount of times you've saved my life since I met
you, are you truly going to try and convince me
that you killed your own mother to save yourself?"

"But I did." I felt like I was choking." I let
them swap—"

"I'm not going to pretend that I know what
happened," he murmured, cutting me off again.
"But whatever did or didn't happen there, you
were a child. You didn't let her do anything. She
chose to protect you." Aleki pressed a kiss to my
temple, settling me while Cillian spoke.

"Renita, please let me take you up." He
murmured, his voice warming some of the cold in
me. "Some sunshine, some food, and somewhere to
rest. Cillian can handle things here."

I wanted to argue. This was my mess. My
skeletons in the closet, but exhaustion once again
made my body ache. Cillian had already released

me, Leonardo and Nyx flanking him to exit the
opened cathedral of the ceiling, and the trio
disappeared before I could find my voice. Mateo
and Juan remained with us, and despite my
exhaustion I released a laugh, knowing I was
officially outnumbered.

"...Anyone else want to add a margarita to
that self-care list?" I asked, earning the smiles
and chuckles I needed. That didn't happen of
course. I was asleep shortly after the sunlight
warmed all the ice from my skin.

I woke up slightly disoriented. I could still
taste salt on my lips, hear the sea breeze and
distant gulls, but I was weighed down where I lay.
A soft huff of breath against the nape of my neck
roused me enough to recognize the weight of
Aleki's arm wrapped around my waist.

Shuffling slightly, I spied Mateo sprawled
across the end of the bed, and Juan tucked into an
armchair across the room. The balcony doors were
open, letting in the sound of waves lapping in the
pale light.

"Feeling better?" Aleki's voice was thick with sleep, and he didn't budge. If anything, he sinched me slightly tighter like he was afraid I would bolt from the bed. I was slightly tempted to.

"A little," I admitted, trying to pry his arm off me. He chuckled against my neck, kissing me once. Twice.

My face began to burn as he continued his lazy perusal, his thumb rubbing slow circles on my hip. I instantly stiffened when he nipped my neck, eliciting another chuckle from him as his hand spread across my navel, pinning my back to his chest.

"Relax little predator. I'll behave myself so long as you don't squirm."

"You'll behave yourself so that I do not retch," Mateo grumbled at our feet. Aleki pushed up on his elbow, frowning over me at the Mer who slowly sat up, making a disgruntled sound. Juan stirred at the sound of his brother's voice, eliciting a dramatic huff from Aleki as he fell back to the bed.

"Fine."

"Where are we?" I asked, wiggling out of his grip and trying to stand despite the migraine splitting my skull in two.

"A resort. Fancy one full of foreigners," Mateo continued to grumble, but was on his feet and by my side within a millisecond. "You should continue to rest, alteza. The effect of the coral is still in your system."

Aleki pats the mattress beside him with a smug grin. I rolled my eyes.

"Where's—"

"Cillian is across the street," Juan piped up, reading my mind. He yawned softly, ignoring the look of betrayal Aleki shot him. "With Cora."

My eyes found Aleki's instantly, and he relented, all playfulness gone. They exited the room only for me to change, which I did in record time. A quick rinse in the shower and then I was dragging on a tank top and jean shorts, bursting into the hallway barefoot while twisting my hair into a bun.

"Whoa, take it easy," Aleki said, smirking at me as he caught me around the waist before I careened into Juan. He frowned down at my bare feet but didn't argue with me. The elevator ride was ripe with my anticipation, nearly making me bounce on my feet. Mateo whispered the name of the bistro across the street, and I took off ignoring the cries of protest at my back.

The sidewalk was hot against the soles of my feet, but I didn't care. The street was mostly deserted as I jogged across it, other than for a few morning cyclists. I spied Cillian's shock of white hair first. He didn't even have time to turn around before my aunt rose from the table and caught me in her arms.

29

Renita

"I would have flown her out last night," Cillian's voice reached me over the sobs rocking my body. "Of course, she was several steps ahead of us though and waiting on the beach for our arrival."

"I know the Mers persistence," Cora quipped past me, reaching up to wipe a tear from my face. "And Renita, I didn't doubt you for a moment. I just wanted to prepare; in case you needed us."

"Us?" I asked, finally catching my breath. I'd held myself together this long, I needed to compose myself. When I caught his eye Cillian looked equally intrigued but remained quiet.

"Oh hell." Cora flopped back down to her seat, picking up a glass of something I'm certain wasn't water considering she giggled to herself. Whatever she was about to share had to have

242

been weighing on her for a long time— she never drank unless she was actually scared.

"Cora?" I prodded, perching in the chair next to her and squeezing her knee, drawing her attention back to me as she finished off her glass.

"Renita you'll have to forgive me sweetheart. I truly didn't mean to keep anything from you but knowing the color of your tail... goddess."

"Miss Lenox, I want to be the first to reassure you that no one is placing blame squarely on your shoulders," Cillian cut in. The others had materialized around us, the twins seated with Nyx and Leonardo a table over. Aleki lowered himself into a chair on Cillian's other side. "We, as well as Renita, just expect full transparency now that she has taken her rightful place." Cora gasped lightly, and I carefully avoided her gaze.

"...Serena," She finally said, composing herself. "Your mother. She knew she had birthed the future Queen before you had even taken your first breath. Everyone in that room did. The aura, your voice when you gave your first cry— there was no mistaking what you were or what you'd become." Tears burned in my eyes, but I refused to let them fall. Cora took my hand, squeezing tightly as she addressed Cillian.

"The witches council has been tasked to aid in protecting your world from outsiders, which included intervening with what rogue Sirens we could. However, we took it upon ourselves to aid them as well." Cillian bristled at my side, violet flickering in my peripheral. I felt each of the Mer lean in slightly. Cora, ever the stubborn mule, carried on unfettered.

"Sirens had nowhere to go once cast out. Many of which were children, who needed guidance to hopefully gain control of their magic before it consumed them whole. Many of them have found solace scattered amongst different Covens, attending our schools, posing as kelpies, cryptids, or other supernatural creatures for their own protection.

"As for the Sirens responsible for hunting you, none of them, at least as far as we know, are linked to any of our networks or schools. Most likely, they were already teenagers or adults when found and cast out. Most likely attacked, which only fueled their fear and hatred of your kind and allowed the darkness in their magic to take root."

"So, you're saying that you've helped build a functioning community of Sirens?" Aleki asked, voice more strained than normal. Cora narrowed her eyes at him.

"I'm saying we took it upon ourselves to raise the children that your kind abandoned. And did a damn well job of it if Renita is any evidence." Aleki clamped his mouth shut audibly, and I couldn't stop a laugh from bubbling out of me.

"You knew from the beginning what I was?" I asked, a small flair of anger rising through the shock of it all. Cora gave me a sympathetic look.

"You lost your mother so young because of your mixture of traits. I did not want to add to the burden by telling you that you were meant to rule on top of…" she trailed off, and my anger quelled. She sighs, leaning back in her seat. "I prayed, and entrusted that in due time, the goddess would set you on the path you needed to be on. That's why I wasn't at all surprised when Cillian himself arrived at our doorstep, rather than sending a noble party to act out his business. The group of you were destined to come together."

She paused, smiling sweetly at a young waiter who appeared out of nowhere to refill her glass, winking as he left. Grinning, she lifted it to her lips, adding, "And if I may be so bold, I personally would love to see you lot heal the rift your own fears have caused."

"That has been my intention for a while now," Cillian said low, our eyes meeting across the table. "I just didn't know how to begin, until now."

Cora clapped her hands together, instantly, her glee dissolving whatever overdramatic heart to heart he was undoubtedly going to try and have with me.

"Well, that is absolutely *wonderful* news indeed! Might I introduce you to Roberta and Desdemona." Cora stood, waving to a table at the far end of the bistro to a pair of women none of us had noticed.

One was a tanned blonde with gleaming blue eyes, and the other sharing my complexion with her dark tresses cut into a short bob. A growl rumbled in Aleki's throat as they approached and Nyx had already stood, but Cillian was looking at them... contemplative.

"Roberta hails from the southeastern coast of New England, is that right?" The blonde nodded, smiling wide enough to show her sharpened teeth. "And Desdemona lives just south of here, close to Sparta." She just nodded, sliding into the chair next to me with a pensive smile.

I blinked once, unsure of what to do. Were they...

"You have no idea the relief we felt when we heard you had survived," Roberta said, confirming my thoughts.

"You're Sirens?" I asked, my free hand instantly finding Cillian's under the table. Nyx hadn't been able to help himself, his hands silently landing on the back of my chair as Roberta scootched her own closer to me.

"We certainly aren't high fae, though we may look the part." Roberta smiled again, her tone making the air ripple as she gazed up at Nyx.

"Control yourself," Desdemona quipped, clearly older and sharing a look with Cora. Then her dark eyes settled on me, softening slightly. "It's good to finally meet you, little cousin." My jaw dropped, and a grin finally curved her lips.

"I'm sorry." Cillian looked downright appalled, paling if he could. "You're cousins?" Desdemona let out a trilling laugh.

"Why yes, young King. We have familial trees just as you do. And before you fret that attractive head of yours," she purred, not even glancing at Aleki as his clenched fist met the table. "I myself am not a royal. Our gifts and tails and laws function irritatingly similar to yours."

Cillian smiled, the same cold smile I'd seen before he turned on his father. "Wasn't a concern that crossed my mind. My concern is how many of you are dotted on this street with a weapon poised at my back."

"None." Cora, scoffed, having finished her second glass. "Do not mix your tainted idea of their kind with the reality."

"It's fine, Cora." Desdemona continued to smile but leaned away slightly to give us space. "Besides Renita here, he's most likely never known a gentle touch from one of us. We can be quite vicious, if provoked."

Despite my burning face, I slapped Aleki on the hand when he bared his teeth and pushed my chair back into Nyx to silence his next growl.

"Get ahold of yourselves. They're not here to fight."

"Force of habit," Leonardo drawled, buried malice in each work as he smirked at Roberta. I sighed heavily. This was going nowhere.

"Would you walk with me?" I asked, both the Sirens turning to me immediately.

"We would not be foolish enough to refuse the company of our Queen," Roberta said, already standing. Desdemona smiled slowly, joining us.

"Nyx, stay with Cillian please," I asked, purposefully keeping my tone light but he tensed up all the same. Finally, he nodded curtly, taking the seat I'd just abandoned. My gaze crossed to the table; meeting Aleki's heated one. "Let's go."

It was still early enough in the day that only locals dotted the beach, still an hour or two before the tourists would take over completely. Or so Desdemona said.

The sun was hot while we walked. Hotter than at home. Here it was dry, and unrelenting. The absence of humidity and the overabundance of salt made my stomach twist with homesickness at the same time it did with a serene sense of calm. Familiarity.

She was studying me as we walked; even though I didn't look at her I could feel her eyes. It was difficult for Aleki to understand what she was explaining, and he wound up interrupting her with questions every few minutes. I though, understood all too well.

Anger. Revenge. Agony. Pain. Loss.

The only thing that humans had been able to comprehend when dealing with such consuming emotions was that depending on the star one was born under, they handled them differently. Cancer, their most emotional sign, was tied to the water. It represented the all-consuming aspect that it was to be a Siren well. To be both an over emotional mess of power and plea, and equally as deadly as the disease which shared the name. It was this comparison which finally helped Aleki understand the depth of what our power demanded. And stole.

For centuries Sirens hid themselves better than any other creature. Practicing. Restraining. Of course, many failed— hence the Mer's understandable concern.

At least in the beginning. It wasn't long before too much was expected. Before Sirens were forbidden from giving into their power at all, and that was the root of the problem. Restraint and suppression were two vastly different things. One exhibited self-control, and the other exhibited self-denial. Unlike a Mer, whose power could only be channeled in one direction, a Sirens power demanded to be channeled through all. It wasn't a simple decision to ignore it, or a choice to not wield it. The longer one went without, the closer to madness one drifted. I myself had drifted on more than one occasion. I understood all that, and was grateful that Aleki found a way to accept it, even if pieces were still confusing to him. That said, I still had a few concerns of my own.

"What of the bloodlust?" I murmured, not meeting anyone's eye. "The urge to kill? The… literal desperation for it."

"Have you given into it?" Desdemona asked, alarm in her tone. I winced, only able to nod. She sighed heavily, running a hand through her hair, holding the dark tresses away from her face as the sea breeze fought to toss them.

"It never truly goes away." We both glanced back at Roberta, who until now had been following behind the three of us in silence. She tossed her platinum hair, still irritatingly stunning. I felt my teeth grinding as she leaned against Aleki. He stiffened but she dared to press her face to his neck, inhaling sharply, sliding her liquid gaze back to mine.

"Mhm… just as I thought. I did not mean to provoke you, my Queen." Desdemona stifled a laugh, offering me a small, handheld mirror that was absolutely made of pure silver.

"Damn it," I grumbled, raising a clawed hand to my cheeks, tracing the dusting of visible scales. Additionally, a glittering ring of green circled my irises. I was shocked to see my ears had pointed as well, taking on a turquoise hue towards the tips.

"Repression causes our more animalistic nature to surface." Roberta giggled, but to my relief extracted herself from Aleki, who dramatically wiped his side as if she dirtied him. "Think of it as the body combating the mind. The more you dip into your true nature, the less all-encompassing it should feel," she explained.

"And what of the numerous Sirens who have been attacking us these past few months," Aleki asked, his tone giving away his restrained displeasure with her. His arms looped around my waist, dragging me against him where she'd been.

"Rogue," Desdemona said, her voice grave. "And as unfortunate as it is to say, lost to their magic. When one goes so far, there is little chance of returning. The only mercy any of us may offer them is a swift death."

A guilt I hadn't known I was harboring instantly soothed, a breath of relief leaving me. I had killed my kind and felt like I had betrayed them in the process. If what Desdemona said was true, whatever functioning society the Sirens had going would have dealt with them similarly for their actions, and lack of control.

"So, you are accountable for the danger you may pose," Aleki said thoughtfully. Desdemona and Roberta shared a smirk.

"Of course we are. We would have ceased to exist by now otherwise. Especially with the Mer's lack of support."

He winced behind me, and I folded my hands over his where they rest on my belly, fingers splaying against his in an attempt to soothe. Like the tide and wind, that would be changing. Cillian alone had already begun forging a new path ahead, and with support, I would be strong enough to follow. As if sensing my inner confirmation on the matter, Desdemona leveled a satisfied smile at me.

"Here." She shifted the small burlap bag she was carrying off her shoulder, extending it to me. Confused at first, I just stared at it, before unzipping it and pulling out a large, midnight blue jewelry box. My stomach flipped, a broken sound leaving me as I whipped the lid open. All my treasures from the river glittered up at me in the light of the morning sun. All my mother's pearls, her comb, my crystal jewelry and the golden coins tourists would toss— everything.

I was at a loss for words, but Desdemona just smiled before she and Roberta turned towards the waves. Their human clothing fell to the sand as they let the sea swallow them up to the chest. I wasn't surprised at all when Roberta shifted, her skin taking on scales of the most serene bay blue. But Desdemona shocked both Aleki and I.

A flash of golden sunrays crisscrossing the water, like honey staining the wave which rolled over her. Like me, scales dotted her warm skin, making it appear even more sun kissed than it was naturally. Her melodic laughter shook me back to my wits.

"You're a priestess?" I asked, finding my voice while Aleki just stared in awe. She smiled wider, fangs glinting in the golden reflection her tail cast across the waves.

"Nearly as rare as you, my sweet cousin. We shall see you again soon." A gentle splash was their parting wave, both disappearing back to the water which we came from.

I drew a shaky breath, unconsciously leaning back into Aleki who was more than happy to accommodate me. His hands smoothed down my arms, his mouth moving against my hair.

"Are you alright?"

"...Yes," I said, letting my eyes drift shut.

I felt the storm raging within me slowly began to quell. The sharp edge of a cliff curbed back to the gentle roll of the sea. The screaming of the wind muted to the call of gulls, and the lapping of the water at my toes. The tide was coming in, reaching for me. And I finally felt steady enough in my skin to reach back for it.

Cillian

"Sleeping again?" I was roused by Alek's teasing prod against my side, his fingers curling just enough to tickle. I knew it was also still his anxiety, needing to check occasionally that my wounds had fully healed. So, I didn't fight him… too much.

I rolled suddenly, catching him by surprise and pinning him to the damp towel laid out beneath him. He'd gone swimming without me while I dozed, which could only mean one thing.

My head whipped up, landing on Renita a few paces away. She lounged in a beach chair, half in the surf, a drink poised in one hand. Her brow arched as she held my stare.

"Well don't stop on my account." A smile curved her lips as they closed around the end of a straw, sipping on whatever drink Mateo had surely made her. He's developed a thing for bartending recently. At least being our personal bartender that is. Something about Martini's never being made right, and our Queen deserves the best.

Aleki rolled his hips up against me, reminding me that he was there and of what I'd been flirting with doing, but I restrained myself. I smoothed his hair back, pressing a kiss to his mouth, before easing myself back on my heels.

"Anyone care to fill me in on what I missed, or will I need to work for it?" Alek's answering grin was wicked, but Renita just silently blushed. The last time I dozed off on 'vacation' I'd wound up being 'punished' by being savored between the two in the process for answers. Perhaps I could get that lucky again.

"Desdemona came by," Renita offered, rising from her chair and I groaned. The pathetic excuse of a bikini she wore was the same shade of red as Alek's scales. He pushed up to sit, yanking her down into his side as she pretended to struggle. We always allowed our Queen to keep her pride but never allowed her to refuse her desires. Both the ones we could satiate, or only support.

"Has she located another colony?" I asked, trying to focus on the topic at hand.

That's what we have been calling the small communities of Sirens we've been locating. Each 'vacation' was centered around an area that based on the witch's intel and Desdemona's ever-growing support, we should be able to find a group or a family managing to get by.

Most were anything but receptive to our presence unless Renita was with us, and I respected that boundary. It wasn't my place to try and undo all the damage the previous Mer royals had dealt. Rather it was my place to be patient and allow things to heal with my support instead of my control.

"Yes. But they've heard of us at least." Her relief was palpable and shared amongst us all. "They're willing to meet. Apparently, their eldest son was born with the tail of a noble, and he's most excited to meet the two of you," she said, a hand landing on either of our arms in a gentle whack.

"A noble Siren?" Alek asked, eyes bright with intrigue. I groaned dramatically.

"Oh lovely. All we need is for you to have an overpowered prodigy."

He made a sound of protest, but Renita was snickering with me, officially outnumbering him. I gazed beyond them finally, checking on the others. Mateo and Juan were tapping a soccer ball between themselves down the beach, trying to teach Leonardo some foot tricks it seemed. However, he was too distracted keeping an eye on Nyx who was seated cross legged in the sand, carefully out of reach of the surf. And the woman lounging within it.

Roberta had insisted on joining us as often as possible, slowly easing her way beyond Nyx's many walls. Though he still refrained from visibly reacting to her presence, I knew him well enough that it was only a matter of time before she successfully coaxed him out from under Leonardos watchful eye.

"I trust her." Renita had followed my gaze, her hand squeezing mine reassuringly. "I actually think she may be good for him."

"Forget him, what's good for me?" Alek fakes a pout, and I glare at him. That look always got him his way, and he smiled smugly over Renita's head as she leans over to place a kiss on his cheek. I follow, a shadow at her back and press a kiss to her own cheek, before releasing a satisfied hum against her skin.

"Mi tesoro…"

"I'm here," she murmured, giving me my own kiss. And goddess, I fell in love all over again.

Acknowledgments.

As always, thank you to my wonderful husband. This story took a different route than my usual ones. So much world building, so my imagery, so much self-inflicted lore. Thank you for helping me wade through the abundance of colors, scents, sights and sounds to bring this gorgeous world to life.

I made so many new bookish friends on this journey. Thank you, Castle Door Wax Melts, for bringing yet another character scent to life! Thank you, MG, for the stunning chapter headers and scene break designs! And thank you, A. J. Knight, for illustrating the cutest little chibi character art I have ever seen! And of course thank you to the numerous author friends who took the time to read through pieces of my drafts to help me make sure I was making sense and balancing the magic and romance of the story out nicely.

Last but certainly not least, thank you to my readers. I hope you continue to find joy in my magical, chaotic little worlds.

With grace, love, and a fair amount of chaos,

Nightshade